## "You're not alone in this."

Cassie stood there looking lost and alone and upset, and there wasn't a damn thing he could do to make her feel better. She'd have to ride out this storm or leave town. She'd already mentioned the possibility herself, a reminder that had left him feeling warned.

Knowing he was being a fool, but doing it anyway, he rose and went to gather her into his arms. The instant he drew her close, he realized he might have just made the biggest mistake of his life….

Dear Reader,

I'm sure most of us have been bullied at one time or another while we were in school, if not later in life, as well. Plenty of us probably remember some of it. I know I still remember a few incidents, especially the time a teacher bullied me. I didn't want to go back to school.

The heroine of this story doesn't realize that she carries scars from when she was bullied in school, and it takes the hero's love to help her past them. What's more, as a teacher now, she is again being bullied by someone hiding in the shadows and threatening her very life.

This is a deeply emotional story about caring, about community and about love. But it's also a story of the darker side of human nature and how we triumph. For me it always comes down to love: how we love each other, both as couples and as community. Love is the best answer we have. Sometimes it's the only answer.

Bullying can leave lifelong scars. And while this story is about love's triumph, it also touches on an issue that we as a community need to deal with. Our kids should not be afraid to go to school.

Hugs,

Rachel

# RACHEL LEE

## Rancher's Deadly Risk

HARLEQUIN®

entertain, enrich, inspire™

Recycling programs
for this product may
not exist in your area.

ISBN-13: 978-0-373-27797-1

RANCHER'S DEADLY RISK

**Books by Rachel Lee**

# RACHEL LEE

was hooked on writing by the age of twelve, and practiced her craft as she moved from place to place all over the United States. This *New York Times* bestselling author now resides in Florida and has the joy of writing full-time.

To all the kids everywhere who live in fear of bullies.
You are not alone.

# Chapter 1

Cassie Greaves felt the winter nip in the Conard County air as she left her small rental house to head for school. The rising sun to the east cast a buttery glow over the world, and the trees that had fully turned a few weeks ago were now shedding their brilliant cloaks, leaving behind gray, reaching fingers. She scuffed her feet through the dry leaves and almost laughed from the joy of it.

For much of her teaching career, all seven years of it, she had taught in much warmer climes, places where there might be only two seasons, or at most three. Part of what had drawn her here was winter, the idea of being cold, of needing to bundle up, and cozy evenings with a cup of something hot as she graded papers or read a book.

Having grown up in the Northeast, she had found a growing desire to need extra blankets at night, to awake some morning and hear the world hushed under a fresh snowfall.

As romantic as her image was, however, she also knew there would be parts she wouldn't exactly enjoy, but this morning she didn't want to think about them.

She wanted to think about that invigorating nip, the possibility of rediscovering her Nordic skis and the school she was coming to enjoy so much. It was smaller than she was used to, only eight hundred students in the entire high school. And even with budget cutbacks, her classes were smaller. It was easier to get to know her students, and she was beginning to recognize most of the faces that walked the hallways.

Hallways. Another thing she liked. At her last few schools, there had been no hallways, only covered walkways, which meant moving from an air-conditioned classroom out into the heat, only to walk into another air-conditioned classroom. At times that setup had its charms, but she actually *liked* having interior hallways again.

She smiled and hummed to herself as she walked the four blocks to the high school. There she taught math for all four grades, which gave her days quite a bit of variety.

It had also taught her some lessons. A lot of her students had no interest in advancing to college. They were planning to take over their parents' business or ranch and she had discovered a need to rewrite math problems in ways that seemed useful to them. Unlike some other places she had taught, many students here weren't content to just do the work because it was required.

Plus, in perfect honesty, the students' backgrounds encouraged her to find meaningful ways of phrasing problems because there was so much homogeneity in the things that concerned them. Her elementary algebra class didn't look blankly at her when she asked them to calculate the storage space needed for a certain number of bales of hay.

They went home, measured the bales—round or oblong, depending—and gave her answers based on a practical exercise. Now how cool was that?

Discovering the volume of a grain silo, working with board feet of lumber, sketching out plans for a shed, figuring out how many acres of pasture for a herd of a certain size—all those things enlivened them. Consequently she was discovering a new love for her subject herself.

Drawing in a deep breath of the chilly air, she decided this place was growing on her even more than she had hoped.

When she arrived on the campus, Lincoln Blair was standing outside. He was the football coach and science teacher, an absolute stud of a man who had so far remained reserved, even unapproachable, although everyone else seemed to like him a lot.

In her mind she had dubbed him "Studley Do-right" because he was appealing enough to make her constantly aware of him, sort of like an itch in her libido. He had dark hair, astonishingly bright blue eyes and there was something about him that always made her think he must have descended from a long line of Celtic warriors. Square-jawed, weathered a bit from sun and wind, with narrow hips he unconsciously canted in a way that made it impossible for a woman not to notice them.

She gathered from things the other teachers had said that he owned a ranch that had been in his family for generations, and he worked it as time allowed, which probably explained that weathered look. Regardless, while most of the teachers had certainly been welcoming enough, his air of reserve truly set him apart.

Not that she should probably blame *him*. She'd had enough experience with men who wanted nothing but a fling with her, and had concluded there must be something essentially wrong with her. On the other hand, she reminded herself that getting involved with a colleague was seldom wise, and in a small town like this, it might even be a wider problem if people noticed and started talking.

Nor was it as if he were the first man who had ever ignored her. Noticing him amounted to a recipe for grief, judging by her past experience.

He nodded as she approached and opened the door for her with a quiet good-morning, but didn't follow her in. She guessed he had bus duty, the job of standing outside to make sure that no one used the space and time between getting off the bus and through the doors to make trouble.

She tried to shake away thoughts of Lincoln Blair from her mind as she passed other teachers with cheery greetings and made her way to her desk. Unlike other schools where she had taught, she had her own classroom, which also provided her with an opportunity to personalize things. It felt nice to have a space where she could hang up posters or set out cool objects for the students to explore a bit. As much as possible she tried to apply math to real life because it *was* part of real life, an important part. The applications were just a bit different and more focused here.

She prepared her desk quickly, then stepped into the hall to monitor arriving students. This school still had homerooms, a place where students went to have their attendance recorded and hear morning announcements, something she hadn't seen since her own school days long ago. Then fifteen minutes later they moved on to their first classes.

In her last few schools, homeroom had been combined with the first class of the day. It might have cut down on movement, but inevitably it cut into the instructional hour one way or another.

Since it was Friday, her students were a little more restless and less focused than usual, their minds on the many things they had planned for the weekend. Or perhaps they were just thinking of escape into absolutely gorgeous weather.

Either way, she felt some fatigue by the time she was able to close her classroom for lunch. She didn't have cafeteria or study hall duty that day, so the teachers' lounge beckoned.

Bag lunch in hand, she entered the corridor flow as some students headed for the cafeteria and others to study hall.

The wing emptied swiftly and before she reached the end of the corridor she was alone. Or thought she was. As she turned a corner and passed the men's bathroom, she heard a shout that made her pause.

"Stop it! Just leave me alone!"

Without even hesitating, afraid that waiting for a male teacher to arrive could allow something bad to happen, she elbowed the door open.

The five students inside didn't even hear the door. The sight instantly disturbed her. She knew every school had its underside, but what she was seeing now horrified her.

One of her best math students, James Carney, was huddled in a corner on the floor, his arms protectively over his face. He was small for his years, and string-bean thin, and she'd already noticed he didn't seem to have many friends, if any.

Four boys stood around him, taunting him with names like nerd, jerk, girlie, sissy…part of her was waiting to hear "fag," but that epithet didn't appear while she stood there taking in the scene.

She didn't need a mental map to know what was going on. Before she could react, two of the boys spat on James and she could tell that wasn't the first time.

Before the scene could get any uglier, she clapped her hands as loudly as she could and shouted, "Stop this now!"

Four startled faces turned her way. It took a little longer for James to lower his arms from his head.

"Just what do you think you're doing?" she demanded. "You shouldn't treat anyone like this, not anyone. Ever. But this is a violation of school policy. You know what the penalty is. James, are you all right?"

The youth jumped to his feet and hurried for the door. "I'm fine," he muttered as he rushed past her. "You're making it worse."

"Go to the nurse," she called after him before turning to face the four others. As the full impact of what she had just seen began to hit, she could feel herself roiling with anger. For long seconds she simply stared at the four young men who had been taunting James. *Keep it cool,* she reminded herself. It was important to stay calm and reasonable.

"Bullying," she said quietly, "is despicable. It shows you to be small men, not big ones. It isn't tolerated by school policy and you know it. You're coming to the principal with me."

"Make us," snarled one of them, then they all brushed past her, bumping her shoulder as they went, leaving her both livid and helpless. She couldn't run out into the hall after them, nor could she physically stop them.

But there was something she could do. She picked up her bagged lunch, tossed it in the trash—she didn't want to eat it after it had fallen to the bathroom floor—and headed for the principal's office herself. None of this was going to be tolerated.

My God, James had looked as if he expected to be beaten…or as if he had been. She just wished she had recognized the other four boys by name. Apparently they were in Teasdale's math classes. Gloria Teasdale was semiretired, teaching only three classes a day. An elderly woman who wore too much perfume, she was sometimes the object of derogatory remarks from her students, but Cassie ignored the comments. Kids would talk about teachers outside the classroom, and she could see no point in stepping down on it. She was no martinet and she was equally certain some of her students had derogatory things to say about her. The nature of the beast, she thought with grim amusement.

But bullying was a whole different matter, damaging to the bullied student emotionally, if not physically, and most definitely against the school's conduct policies.

She reached the office and asked Marian, the front desk receptionist and secretary, to call the nurse's office and find out if James was okay. Then she joined the principal in his small office. He always ate lunch at his desk, eschewing both the teachers' lounge and the cafeteria.

Sometimes she thought of him as barricaded away from all the possible disturbances in a high school. At other times she thought he just felt like a fish out of water, not sure of his welcome even in the faculty lounge. Or maybe he just thought people would be more comfortable if he wasn't around. She didn't have a good read on him yet.

His round face smiled as he greeted her. He was about fifty pounds overweight, and his lunch consisted of a few slices of lean chicken over a bed of fresh vegetables. He had confided that he was dieting without much success. She looked at that lunch and felt a pang of sympathy.

"Still starving?" she asked him.

"Unfortunately. The doc says I've lost two pounds, though, so I guess it's working. Some days I'm not sure it's worth it."

"I can imagine."

He leaned back, ignoring the dry salad and chicken in front of him, a meal that cried out for a little salad dressing or mayonnaise to help it go down. "Is something wrong? You look…disturbed." He waved her to the seat in front of his desk.

She sat, trying to gather her thoughts, trying to maintain a calm she was far from feeling. "I am upset," she admitted. "I saw an instance of bullying in the boys' room. I stopped it, but when I tried to bring the bullies to you, they told me I couldn't make them and they brushed past me. Les, you know bullying is a violation of the conduct code."

"How bad was it?"

"They were spitting on him and calling him names. He was cowering on the floor in a corner as if he expected to be hit or kicked."

He frowned. "That's bad. That's very bad. All of it. Who were they after?"

"James Carney."

He shook his head. "I can't say I'm surprised. Some people just seem to draw that kind of attention."

"All it takes is being a little different."

"And James is certainly that. Smarter than most, small. Did you know he skipped a grade last year? I don't think that's helped him any but his parents and a committee of teachers felt we couldn't hold him back. Maybe we should have."

"We shouldn't have to," she argued, getting a little hot. "That boy should be free to move ahead if he's capable without four other boys attacking him for it."

Les nodded slowly. "Can you identify the bullies?"

"By face, not by name. They must be in Mrs. Teasdale's math classes."

"If they're still in math at all." He sighed. "How would you prefer to handle it?"

"The rules call for suspension," she reminded him. When he didn't answer immediately, she started to feel both annoyed and nervous. Surely he wasn't going to propose they simply ignore this?

Marian stuck her head in the door. "James Carney never went to the nurse." Then she popped out again.

"So he must be all right," Les remarked.

"That doesn't make this all go away!"

Les lifted his brows and held up a hand. "I didn't say that. I'm just relieved the Carney boy is okay."

"*Physically* okay," Cassie said almost sarcastically. "I'm sure I don't need to educate you on the other effects of bullying."

"Of course not." He sounded almost sharp. "I'm as well-informed as you on the subject. That's why it's against our code of conduct."

She tried to dial back her irritation. "I'm sorry. It just upset me, and then when they defied me that way, I got even more concerned. If they're not going to listen to a teacher, how are we going to stop this? And what are we going to do about it?"

Les leaned forward, shoving his lunch to one side. He rested his forearms on his desk. "I don't think suspensions would be prudent, not yet."

"What?" She was horrified and still sickened by what

she had seen. "We can't just ignore this. And we can't ignore the rules if we expect them to have any force."

"Just hold on a minute and calm down a bit. I understand you're upset and I understand why. You have every reason to be upset. But this isn't a big-city school. I don't favor zero tolerance for a very good reason. Kids will be kids…."

She started to open her mouth but he waved her to silence.

"Just hear me out, Cassie. I'm not excusing what they did. It was wrong. No question. No argument. But we have to ask ourselves what will be the best way to handle this with the least amount of damage."

It took her a moment and a deep breath, but finally she relaxed. "Okay, I'm listening."

"We aren't going to tolerate bullying. You and I agree on that. But we have to ask ourselves how much damage we might do with our response. You must have noticed by now that not many of our students go on to college. Some of that is because they have the family business waiting for them the day they graduate. Some is because folks simply can't afford it. We have a handful who get scholarships and an equally small handful who can afford it. Most of our students who get any further schooling do it at the local community college."

She nodded. All of this had been explained at the time she was hired.

"So we have to ask ourselves," Les said patiently, "whether we want to do something that might make a student choose to drop out, or that might damage a student's ability to get a college scholarship. We've got a couple, I'm sure you know, who are poised to get athletic scholarships. Suspension would take that away."

It was then that she made a mental connection and knew who one of the bullies was. "One of them was our star basketball forward."

Les lowered his head. "Cripes. Now you're talking about the state championship and a boy's entire future. He's looking good to get a basketball scholarship. Recruiters have been here several times."

"He should have thought of that before he started bullying James Carney."

"I agree. But he's still seventeen. You remember being that age? How many times did you think things through, especially when you were with a group of people your age? That's what bothers me about zero tolerance. Why wreck any kid's life if we can handle it another way?"

Cassie bit her lip. She wasn't exactly a fan of zero tolerance herself, understanding that young people made mistakes almost as naturally as they breathed. "But this is a little different," she argued. "This was no mistake. Four of them ganged up on one student. I don't know how far they might have gone if I hadn't barged in. And we have to consider James Carney and what this might do to him."

"I am considering it," Les said. "I want it stopped, but I don't want it to result in additional bullying or anybody's life being wrecked."

"So what will you do?"

"You identify those students. I'll call their parents and make it clear that if this happens again they will be suspended. In the meantime I'll give them detention."

Cassie felt sickened, yet she couldn't rightly argue with what he proposed. He *was* right. They had to be careful not to inflame the situation, and take care that they didn't cause students to drop out or lose scholarships, unless this continued.

"You're not happy," Les remarked. He poked at his lunch listlessly then ignored it again. "I understand. I'm not happy, either. We've always had some minor bullying—what school doesn't? But I don't think we've ever had an incident as bad as what you're describing, at least not in my memory. If you've got a better solution, let me know. Just understand, there are no perfect solutions. If I bring the hammer down too hard, that could result in James being bullied worse. We've got to try to reason our way through this to cause the least damage to all five of those students."

She said nothing, feeling her stomach sinking but unable to argue against his logic. "I hate bullying," she said finally. "It damages the victim well past the incident, sometimes for life. What's more, I hate the thuggish mentality of those who do it."

"Then maybe we need to do something about the mentality. It's not enough to just put a ban on it in the code. Maybe we need to use this as an instructional opportunity."

She perked a little at that statement. "How so?"

"We need to educate our students, maybe their families. We need them to truly understand how bad this is."

She nodded. "What those boys were doing could get them arrested."

It seemed to her that Les blanched a bit. "Oh, let's not go that far. Criminal records for assault? Battery, if it happened?"

"I don't want to do that, either," she agreed. "I'm just saying, if we can't get through with an emotional appeal to a sense of fair play and what's right, we could also list the criminal consequences. Bring it home. Maybe have a law enforcement officer tell them a few things."

Les smiled. "I can see you already have ideas. So what

I'd like is for you to get together with another teacher and come up with a plan for an assembly or two."

Cassie's mind immediately skipped ahead and was already summoning ideas for the assembly and maybe a long-term program. "Okay. Who do you suggest I work with?"

"Linc Blair. He's the most popular teacher with the students and seems to carry a lot of moral authority with them." Les gave a little laugh. "More than I do, certainly. Yes, I'll explain the situation to Linc at the end of the day and see if he's willing. In the meantime, try to get the bullies' names for me. I want to spend some time on the phone with parents."

He paused. "God, I hope this isn't resulting from things that are happening to these boys at home."

It could well be, Cassie thought as she left his office a few minutes later. Bullies were sometimes created.

Why did she feel as if she might be about to overturn a rock and discover some ugly things?

If there was any upside to this at all, she supposed it was that she would at last find out why Lincoln Blair avoided her as if she had the plague.

By close of school that day, she had the names of the four bullies. She had asked for the aid of other teachers, without explaining why she needed to know. List in hand, she headed for Les's office and found he was already talking to Linc. He waved her in to join them and she took the second chair that faced Les's desk.

"Cassie here can give you more detail," Les said, "given that she's the one who broke it up."

She looked at Linc and noted the way those startling blue eyes of his met hers then swiftly looked away.

"I have the students' names," she said quickly, passing her list to Les.

He took it almost as if it might bite him, then muttered a word no teacher was allowed to use within the school. "Ben Hastings," he said. "Damn, why did it have to be Ben?"

"He never struck me as the bullying type," Linc remarked.

Cassie started to bristle. "I didn't make up the names."

Linc glanced her way again. "I didn't say you did. I'm just surprised. As high a profile as he has because of his basketball skills, I would have thought that if he were a bully we'd have known long ago. That's all I meant."

Cassie caught herself, realizing that she was taking everything too personally. She'd been upset about James all afternoon, and if she were honest, she suspected some of that had to do with some bullying she had endured when she'd been a plump adolescent. Boys and even some girls had picked on her weight mercilessly.

"As far as I know," Les said, "the worst cases of bullying we've had in the district have been in the elementary and middle schools. A few fights, name-calling, some blows. But it seems to get better by this age. Or at least less extreme."

"Things have changed," Linc remarked. "We got a lot of new people in town when the semiconductor plant opened, and even after the layoffs there are still a lot of students who didn't grow up around here. That creates a different kind of tension."

Les lifted a brow. "In what way?"

"Outsiders versus insiders. It used to be most of these incidents could be worked out between families who had a stake in keeping things friendly. It's not like that anymore, and new kids make obvious targets. James Carney is a new kid, for one thing, despite the fact he was born here. The family just moved back after years away. He's also a serious student, he's small and he isn't involved in sports. Very much an outsider. He makes easy pickings for a pack."

"So what are you saying?"

Linc leaned forward. "I'm saying we have to nip this in the bud. We can't allow serious bullying to go unchallenged or we'll have more of it. I get why you're reluctant to suspend these students. Hell, it'll probably just make the whole thing worse for James Carney, and maybe even for Ms. Greaves here."

"Cassie," she said automatically, as she waited to hear where he was taking this.

"Cassie," he repeated with barely a glance in her direction. "Look, Les, we have a different dynamic now from anything we're used to around here. We've got new kids, new ones who don't have to go home at night and help in the family ranch or business. Kids who are, relatively speaking, on easy street. They get fancy electronics, most have newer cars, and if they take jobs it's for pin money. What makes you think that isn't going to breed resentment?"

Les's frown had deepened and Cassie felt her stomach turn over. Under no circumstances did she want to see another incident like she had today. The memory still sickened her, the sight of James cowering and those boys spitting on him.

"I've been watching the changes take hold," Linc continued. "A lot of the new kids are going to go to college. They're not going to stay here. The other students know it. Outsiders just passing through. We've been having more and more instances of division, separate groups forming, and some name-calling. Why the hell else do you think I have a zero-tolerance policy on bullying for my football players? I never used to need one, but I've made it clear over the last couple of years that one instance of bullying is enough to get a player thrown off the team."

"You're not proposing we suspend all these students!"

"Not yet," Linc said quietly, sitting back. "But your idea of starting an antibullying program is a good one. We've got to educate before this gets out of hand. And it will get out of hand. The bullying won't just be going in one direction, either. The factions have been forming. We can't let the divisions get any deeper or uglier."

As she listened, Cassie got an inkling of why Linc was so well-liked and respected by students and faculty alike. He seemed to truly have his finger on the pulse of this school.

"How do you know all this?" she asked.

"I pay attention. My students talk to me." He gave her the briefest of smiles. "I've been around a while, too. It's easier for me to see what's happening than it would be for you, or even for Les. He doesn't have as much student interaction as I do."

"So we start a program?" she asked.

"Definitely. As for what happened today, I'm concerned. It's one thing when you see this among third graders or even seventh graders. But these students are on the cusp of adulthood. In the spring or in another year they're going to walk out of here men. They should be past this by now. Sure, they might have little shoving matches, or call a name or two when they get annoyed, but this kind of ganging-up should be well behind them. We're going to have to tread carefully so we don't make things worse."

Cassie spoke. "So you agree with the way Les wants to handle it?"

"We have to do *something*. From the minute you walked in on it, from the instant they ignored your authority as a teacher, we haven't had a choice. There has to be a statement made, punishment doled out. We can't let anyone think they can get away with any of that. But I'd really like it if we could find a way that wouldn't cause more grief for James Carney."

"He didn't do anything," Cassie said. "He wouldn't even talk to me. In fact, he said I was making it worse. If they want to be mad at someone, it should be me."

Les spoke. "We can make the detentions about the way they treated Ms. Greaves and nothing else."

Linc looked at her, really looked at her, for the first time, and she felt an electric shock all the way to her toes. "How *did* they treat you exactly?"

"Well, it wasn't just that they wouldn't come with me to the principal's office. When they passed me to get out the door, they made sure to bump into me, and it wasn't exactly just brushing by."

Linc's dark brows lifted. "That's definitely not good."

Les slapped his hand on the desk. "We can't let that pass under any circumstances. We'll have anarchy."

"But this isn't about me," Cassie protested.

"It is now," Linc answered. "You just got bullied, too." He sighed. "Okay, this is how I see it. Leaving out the gruesome details for now, put the bullies on detention for ignoring Ms. Greaves—Cassie. Make it about ignoring a teacher's direction. We'll get to the rest of it as we go, but for now let's take the spotlight off James Carney. Maybe they'll duck and leave him alone since he won't be the source of their headache for the time being."

Cassie turned the incident around in her mind, remembering the way those students had bumped her shoulder on their way out. It had been a little more than disrespectful. Almost like a hinted threat. Linc was right, *she* had been bullied, too. A little flicker of anger started burning in the pit of her stomach.

"I don't want to make Cassie an inadvertent target," Les said.

Cassie shifted in her chair. "Look, Les, we can't let this go. What do you think those students will do to me, anyway? They can get as mad as they want. Surely you aren't suggesting they'd physically hurt me."

Les looked shocked. "No, of course not. You're a *teacher*."

Cassie didn't think that was much protection, but on the other hand she figured these students wouldn't want the veritable hell that would come their way if they treated her the way they had treated James.

Linc spoke. "Just make it clear to them that it's unacceptable to ignore a teacher, and then add something about how touching her, so much as *touching,* however briefly, is a crime called battery. I don't think any of them is stupid enough to ignore that."

"I agree," said Cassie. "Let's get this program going, give the students detention for ignoring me, call their parents about their behavior and see how much help you'll get. Keeping the spotlight off James is the best thing to do. I don't want them turning on him any more than they already have. He's the one in most need of protection."

"Okay then." Linc rose from his chair, an almost iconic figure in old jeans, cowboy boots and a faded chambray shirt. "I've got to get to the locker room again before the team wonders if I fell off the edge of the planet. We have an away game tonight." Then he turned his attention to Cassie. "Are you okay with this? Really?"

"Being the center of the storm? Of course. Those bullies don't frighten me, they make me mad."

One corner of his mouth ticked up in a smile. "I'll give you a call tomorrow morning and we'll set up some meeting time to get this ball rolling."

He strode out, and Cassie's gaze followed him helplessly. Wow, she thought, he was going to call her. Maybe she didn't stink as bad as she sometimes thought. Les called her attention back.

"If you're okay with this, then that's how we'll handle the matter for right now. But not for too long. I don't want those students to think they're going to get away with bullying anybody."

"I couldn't agree more." Finally feeling satisfied with the direction they were taking, she said goodbye to Les, picked up her book bag and headed out for the weekend.

The day was still glorious, although twilight wasn't far away. Winter nights came a lot earlier up here than she was used to.

But instead of thinking about the glorious weather or the relaxing weekend ahead, she was thinking about Linc Blair again. Dang, he almost acted like it hurt to even look at her. Had she turned ugly since yesterday?

Shaking her head, she tried to think of other things. Despite her reaction in the principal's office, she wasn't entirely easy about transferring the bullies' anger toward her.

She had taught in a school where a teacher had been attacked by a student, and she didn't labor under any delusions that her status protected her. On the other hand, bullies were usually cowards at heart.

It would be okay, she assured herself.

But it would be even nicer to know why Linc seemed so determined to keep such an obvious distance. He didn't even make the normal friendly overtures to her, like the other teachers.

No, it was as if he, or she, were surrounded by some kind of repulsion field. *Keep away* seemed to bristle all over him.

It probably hurt more than it should have because of her bad experiences in the past. Guys seemed attracted to her just long enough to find out if she was willing to jump in the sack with them, and then either way they made a fast exit. It was, one of her friends admitted, weird. But the same friend had reminded her that dating was a series of "noes" followed by one "yes," eventually.

But never before had she met a guy who seemed to see poison every time his gaze scraped over her and then headed elsewhere.

Not that it mattered, she reminded herself. He was just another guy, albeit one who got her hormones racing every time she looked at him. But just another guy.

And maybe the problem wasn't her at all. After all, he had said he would call her tomorrow about the bullying program.

No, maybe it wasn't her at all.

With that hopeful thought in mind, she hurried home to start dinner and get to the homework papers she needed to check. With any luck, all she'd have left to do by tomorrow was some lesson planning.

The thought brightened her mood a bit, easing the memory of the way James Carney had been cowering.

They were going to help him, and other bullied students. Wasn't that all that really mattered?

## Chapter 2

Linc headed home after the game. It was late because the next high school was so far away, a major problem for running athletics in this part of the country. Ordinarily they avoided night games because of the travel time involved, but this week had been different because the other high school had some construction work going on over the weekend.

They'd gotten their usual shellacking at the other school's hands, though. Nothing different there. Busby somehow always managed to field a stellar team.

But, as he kept telling his players, winning wasn't the point. Playing the game was. As long as they loved to play, the rest didn't matter. Sometimes he wondered if they believed him. Regardless, he always had plenty of students turn up for spring tryouts.

But after he shepherded them off the buses and toward their waiting parents, making sure everyone got a ride home, he still had a forty-five-minute drive of his own to his ranch, and some animals waiting for him.

The sheep and goats were okay in their fenced meadows, watched by the dogs, who were probably wondering by now when they'd see their next bowl of kibble. He had a couple of horses in a corral he never left out overnight, but always safely stalled in the barn. It wouldn't take him long, but he was beginning to feel weary. He started his days at five in the morning, taking care of livestock, and finished at one-thirty in the morning…well, he was getting damn tired.

As the noise of the game and the racket from the players on the team bus began to fade from his immediate memory, along with a running analysis of how the team could improve, Cassie Greaves popped up before his eyes.

Damn, that woman was stunning. Not in a movie-star sort of way, but more like a…a what? Earth mother? She was full-figured enough to qualify, he supposed, though he wouldn't classify her as heavy. No, she was luxuriously built, exactly the kind of female form that had always appealed to him. With bobbed honey-blond hair and witchy green eyes, she was a looker. Every time he glanced at her, he felt swamped by desire. Amazing, almost like he was in high school himself.

But he'd lived his entire life in this county, and he knew how many people came here, thinking they'd found something wonderful, and then after one winter packed up and left because of the cold, the isolation, the lack of excitement. Hell, even people who grew up here left so why wouldn't people who didn't have any roots?

Some people didn't find enough excitement in days filled with work or with people they saw every day. His own fiancée had headed out after just two years here, swearing she would die from boredom. She probably would have, too, he had finally admitted. Who wanted a life with a guy who was either tied up at his job or working a ranch? Much fun he was.

So he just tried to avoid the whole thing. When it came to a woman who attracted him the way Cassie did, a woman who hadn't even survived her first winter here, his guard slammed up like some kind of shield in a science fiction movie.

But he was getting to the point of appearing rude, and that had to stop. When Les had asked him to work on this project with her, he'd had the worst urge to refuse. Proximity with *that* woman?

But then his better angels had taken over. He and Cassie had to deal with this bullying before it got any worse. And it would if they didn't find a way to get through to these students. Ignoring it because "kids will be kids" was a recipe for serious problems. Yes, they'd do it. Most of them probably had bullied at one time or another, and most had probably been the victims of it.

But the problem still couldn't be ignored. That was one thing educators and psychologists had learned over the last few decades. And with the dynamic he'd been watching develop between the students, he suspected that it could get way out of hand.

As the incident had today. As upset as he was for the Carney kid, he also saw a big danger in the way those boys had treated Cassie. So he'd bite the bullet, keep his guard up and do what he could to get the students to understand that bullying wasn't funny, it wasn't a joke, and it was never permissible.

He was glad, though, to reach his ranch and deal with the dogs and the horses. They centered him, these animals he kept. Reminded him he was part of nature, too, and that a lot of nature was actually prettier than human nature.

After he'd greeted, petted, stabled and fed, he went inside and made himself a bowl of instant oatmeal. It had been a long time since dinner, and while team parents made sure there were plenty of snacks and water for the players, he was usually too uptight to eat at all during a game. He was like a father with thirty sons on the field or bench.

Sitting at the kitchen table, eating his solitary oatmeal, he noticed for the first time in a long time just how silent the house was. He'd noticed it after his father had died eight years ago, and he'd noticed it again when Martha had left her engagement ring on this very table.

Silence, usually a good companion given his busy days, sometimes seemed lonely and empty. Tonight it definitely felt empty.

This big old house had been meant for a large family. Built back around the turn of the twentieth century, he had only to look at old family photos to know how full it had been at one time. His great-grandfather must have kept awfully busy expanding the place as well as running the ranch and farm. But after the Second World War, youngsters had moved away. The G.I. Bill had offered them different opportunities, and only his own grandfather had chosen to remain after returning from the South Pacific.

So the old days of a dozen kids had trailed away, his grandmother had born only one child that survived, and then his own mother had died giving birth to him, and his dad had never remarried.

From many to just him. Sometimes when he walked around and counted dusty, empty bedrooms, and imagined what this place might have been like in its heyday, he felt the lack of human contact. Five years ago he'd tried a family reunion, met some of his great-uncles and cousins he hardly knew, and some he'd never met, and after a rush of "we have to keep in touch" from everyone, keeping in touch had ended when they left town. They felt no ties to this place, or to him.

He didn't blame them for that. Time had moved on, and with it so had their lives, which were so far removed now from this thinly populated county that he was sure most of them couldn't imagine why he remained.

But his roots were very real to him. He felt them dig deeper every time he walked the land, or tended to his livestock, or even did a repair around the house. He was a man of this land and he wanted no other.

Martha couldn't grasp it, either, although for a while she had tried. He just hadn't guessed how hard she was trying. Maybe it had been easier for her when everything was new and fresh. Then it had become all humdrum and endless for her, a routine that never changed. He supposed he was to blame for at least some of that, but the fact was, he had two jobs, one teaching, the other tending this place, and he couldn't simply ignore either one. Animals needed daily care. A teaching job required hours not only at school, but also in the evenings and on weekends.

All work and no play apparently had made Linc a very dull boy, he thought. He needed, he supposed, to find a woman from around here who understood the demands and isolation, someone who could be self-sufficient in more ways than Martha. Someone who would be willing to lend her shoulder to the ranch work and make it part of her life, too.

So far no luck. Judging by his attraction to Cassie Greaves, that was most likely his own fault. He never seemed to be drawn to women who had lived here all their lives. Maybe that was his own form of looking for something different. Whatever, it had left his life very empty.

He rinsed his bowl and spoon and put them in the dishwasher Martha had insisted he install. It was a bit much for just one person, and he could go a week without running it, but it was convenient when he didn't feel like washing up after himself. There were days like that, days that were just too long for one reason or another, especially during football season.

Upstairs after his shower, he stood naked in his chilly bedroom and looked out over the moon-drenched fields. There were no curtains any longer. Martha had taken down the ones that had been there at least since his mother had hung them, and replaced them with something she considered cheerier. She hadn't been gone long when he ripped them down and got rid of all the other reminders.

A childish act, part of him judged, but necessary. He didn't need reminders greeting him everywhere he went. Not reminders of Martha, anyway.

The air was getting downright frigid, but he ignored an impulse to turn on the heat. Once he climbed beneath the quilts he'd be warm enough for the night. In the morning he'd deal with seeing his breath and having to dress quickly in clothes that felt as if they'd been in a freezer all night.

Conservation. He preached it to his students, and practiced it himself. Like the compost pile out near the barn. Nothing wasted. He'd been raised that way, and rightfully so. So had many of his students, though not all.

He figured he had a good life in all, and was achieving some good ends, mostly. But nights like this, when the moon was full and the house so silent, he felt he could howl at the moon for a mate. Man was not meant to be solitary.

He shook his head at the turn of his thoughts and went to climb beneath the heap of quilts on his bed, quilts made by generations of women in his family. Heat tomorrow, he decided as his skin met icy sheets. Definitely. He was not going to be a happy camper come morning.

He shivered for a while until his cocoon warmed up. Closing his eyes against the bright moonlight, he thought again of Cassie Greaves. Why did she have to be such a tempting armful?

But surely he knew better now. Nevertheless, thoughts of Cassie seemed to warm that cocoon of quilts faster than usual.

Cassie awoke in a better frame of mind than when she had gone to bed the night before. As awful as the bullying she had seen had appeared to be, she was confident that with some education and a reminder of penalties they could probably lessen the problems.

And giving the boys detention for how they had ignored her should help remove James from the firing line. They would know it all had to do with what they had been doing to James, but with the detentions arising from their treatment of her, they'd have nothing to add to their scorecard against James. She hoped.

By the time she was eating her yogurt and drinking her coffee, she felt good about the program Les had proposed, even though she and Linc hadn't started to work on it. In her experience, the important thing was to create a culture among students, and if possible among their parents, that frowned on bullying. So the question was not whether it would work, but how long it would take.

From what Linc had said yesterday, she gathered there had been a major change in dynamics owing to the new people who had moved here with the semiconductor plant. She'd already heard that sad story of boom and bust. While the plant hadn't closed down when the recession hit, it had laid off quite a few people. A lot of lives had undoubtedly been hurt or destroyed.

But on the other hand, whatever had brought about the social dichotomy in the school, this wasn't the first time she had seen it. Sometimes it was about race. Sometimes it was about who was a "townie" and who was a "military brat." Sometimes it was just about how you dressed and who you hung around with. Kids could find ample reasons to form cliques and exclusive groups. It seemed to be part of human nature in general.

But it could be contained and controlled. Courtesy, which she thought of as the grease on the wheels of life, could be learned, and could overlay baser impulses.

The problem would be one of motivation.

She hoped Linc would have some idea of what would motivate these students, because she didn't know the student body well enough yet and this was a rather late point in their education to start something that should have begun in the earliest grades.

Linc again. She supposed it would be wise to castigate herself for wasting so much thought and energy on thinking about a man who was making it as plain as day that he'd prefer not to get to know her even casually. Work with her? Yes. Anything else, not so much.

Still, she couldn't help wandering into the bedroom to look at herself in the full-length mirror, something she usually avoided. She was plump, yes, but much as she would have liked to be built like a model or movie star, that wasn't in her genetic makeup. She didn't think she looked *that* bad, anyway. Plenty of guys had made passes at her. Full-figured but not ugly was her pronouncement. Problem was, she didn't quite believe the "not ugly" part.

Stifling a sigh, she bathed and dressed in a flannel shirt and jeans, caught her hair up in a short ponytail, and dug out her planning books. Yesterday had pretty much driven everything else out of her mind, and she needed to come up with some kind of new, hands-on project that would teach math in a real-world way.

It had, she admitted, been easier to come up with things at the start of the year, but as the weeks passed, ideas had become thinner on the ground. She scanned the topics to be covered that week, seeking some fertile soil. Unfortunately, she didn't think most of her students were quite ready to enjoy math for the sake of math.

She was searching around on her computer looking for ideas that might work with at least some of what she would teach this week, when the phone rang. She answered, her heart lifting a bit, expecting to hear Linc's voice.

Instead what she heard was a deep, angry voice. "Stay out of what doesn't concern you, bitch, or you'll pay."

Before her jaw could even drop, the other party had disconnected. At once she pressed the caller ID button, but it told her only that the call had come from Wyoming. Great help.

She sat there, staring at her phone, shaken. Just words, she told herself. Just an empty threat. But she couldn't quite persuade herself of that. Her stomach kept flipping nervously, and she'd have given just about anything to call back and give that man a piece of her mind. It would have relieved her anxiety just to be able to yell at him.

Just as anger began to seriously overtake uneasiness, the phone rang again. Without even looking to see who it was, she snapped, "What?"

There was a pause. Finally Linc's familiar voice said, "Cassie?"

At once embarrassment filled her. "Sorry," she said, aware that her voice had thickened, "I just got a nasty call. I thought it was another one."

A moment of silence. "What kind of nasty call?"

"Telling me to stay out of things that don't concern me, with an implied threat and a bit of name-calling. It's nothing, it just made me mad."

He didn't reply directly. "Are you going out?"

"No, I'm doing my weekly planning."

"I'll be there in forty-five minutes."

Then he was gone, leaving her to wonder what had lit the fire under him. Surely the call, as annoying as it had been, didn't require immediate action. Heck, she didn't even know for sure what it was about.

Then it struck her that Linc was on his way over. She hurried into her bedroom and changed into something more attractive than the baggy clothes she had been working in. Nothing too much, just a more attractive blouse with a pair of reasonably new jeans. Another brushing of her hair, a tiny—just tiny—dab of makeup around her eyes and some gloss on her lips.

Then she started a fresh pot of coffee, since somehow she had managed to drink most of it while working this morning. That much caffeine? It struck her that that might have caused the stomach flips as much as the phone call.

She threw open a window to let in some of the fresh, chilly air, then tried to return her attention to her planning. It didn't work. All she could think about was Lincoln Blair coming here. Imagining him walking through her door. Wondering how he would be able to keep up that shield he seemed so determined to place between them while they were working on a project.

God, was she really thinking like this at the age of thirty? That man had truly gotten to her, yet what did she really know about him? That he looked good enough to model on a magazine? That he was popular with both faculty and students?

That meant nothing, really. Nothing. She gave herself a firm mental shake and told herself to remember that she was simply going to be meeting him to work on a project, something she had done countless times before with teachers she found attractive or not-so attractive. So what the hey?

Despite her best efforts, she couldn't help being a little nervous anyway. If he arrived here packed in his personal brand of refrigerant, she didn't know how she would manage. Yes, she had worked with difficult people before, but there was difficult and then there was *difficult*.

Cussing silently, she waited for her doorbell to ring, giving up hope of focusing on her work. Instead she looked around her little office, the house's one spare bedroom, and decided she liked what she had so far been able to do with it. Little by little she was transforming the place into a home that reflected her love of bright color and handmade crafts. Some items she had brought with her, and some she had discovered since arriving here, at a little hole-in-the-wall place that seemed left over from an earlier century.

Finally Linc arrived. Butterflies fluttered wildly in her stomach as she went to open the door.

Her memory had not exaggerated his Celtic-warrior good looks, not one bit. He stood there in a light jacket, jeans and his usual chambray shirt—it was almost a uniform. On his head sat a felt cowboy hat that looked as if it had seen better days.

"Howdy," he said.

His deep voice seemed to pluck a string inside her and make it vibrate. She very nearly forgot to invite him in, then realized she was in danger of standing there like a starstruck kid.

"Come on in," she said. "You didn't have to race over here, you know." Not that she was exactly objecting.

"Probably not, but we needed to meet anyway." He stepped inside and looked around her cozy living room. He surprised her with his choice of words. "Very inviting," he said approvingly.

"That's what I hope," she said as she closed the door behind him. "Coffee?"

"Love some."

He followed her into the kitchen, and as naturally as if he belonged here, he pulled out a chair at her dinette and sat. She filled two mugs, vaguely remembering from school that he liked his black.

"We could go to my office in the back," she suggested.

"This is fine for now."

As if he didn't want to get any deeper into her life or her house. Feeling a bit stung, she placed his coffee in front of him and sat facing him.

"So I started thinking about this program," she began.

He shook his head a little. "In a minute, Cassie. First I want to hear more about that phone call."

As if a switch flipped in her head, she heard that angry, deep voice again. "What's there to say? I told you what he said. He sounded angry, and threatening, but it was just a phone call. It's easy to make anonymous threats."

"It may be easy, but it's seldom pointless. Somebody's

angry with you, and I doubt that many people know yet about what happened yesterday. The boys involved, maybe their parents if Les has already called them all. Maybe a few people they talked to."

She shook her head. "Nothing has happened. Nobody has been suspended. If this stops, nobody *gets* suspended. Scholarships are protected and so is the almighty state championship. If anyone hoped for anything from that call, it's that I wouldn't push this into a suspension."

He set his mug down. "I agree. Essentially. What's troubling me is the way you got treated yesterday. Your authority was ignored, you were pushed, not just brushed by, and now today a threatening call. That incident yesterday was unusually aggressive for students that age. I'm not saying they never get past name-calling and the occasional spat, but like I said yesterday, by this age they're mostly past ganging up and getting physical. Add that to the way they treated you and I'm concerned, that's all."

She thought it over for a moment. "Then maybe I'm not the best choice to help with this antibullying campaign. If I'm seen as just a troublesome outsider, the message may be lost."

"You're not doing this alone," he reminded her.

No, she wasn't. She had tried to avoid meeting his gaze directly, but now she did, and felt as if she were falling into the depths of the incredible blue of his eyes. An almost electric spark seemed to zap her.

Then he broke eye contact, returning his attention to his mug. "I spent some time this morning exploring the subject," he said. "Unfortunately, I have a dial-up connection out there and the internet moves like molasses."

"I've got broadband. We can use my computer."

"Or go to the school."

She sensed he wanted to be out of her house and into a more neutral environment as quickly as possible. Again she felt that sting, but did her best to ignore it. No point creating a Shakespearean tragedy in her own mind.

"Sure, if you want," she said quickly. "Let me get my jacket."

Five minutes later, with a couple of her travel mugs filled with coffee for the two of them, they stepped outside into a brisk morning. Fluffy white clouds raced overhead in a cerulean sky.

"God, it's beautiful here," she said.

"Really?"

She glanced at him. "Don't tell me you don't notice."

"Well, I actually do, especially out at my ranch." For the first time he cracked a genuine smile.

It almost took her breath away. Of course she'd seen him smile on occasion around school, but never had the full wattage been directed her way. Warmth drizzled through her all the way to her toes, and she had to fight to collect her thoughts.

"What do you raise?" she asked as he helped her into his battered pickup, a truck that might have once been a bright red, but now was dulled with age and liberal applications of touch-up paint.

"Actually my dogs do the raising," he said humorously as he climbed in behind the wheel. "They do a damn good job of looking after my sheep and goats. And I have a few horses. It's not much, but it's all I can handle while I'm teaching."

"Why do you keep on doing it?"

"I enjoy it, for one thing. For another, that place has been in my family for over a hundred years. I'm not going to be the one to give it up."

She could understand that, although it was hard to imagine. "You must feel a lot of loyalty."

A faint smile this time, directed out the windshield as he drove toward the school. "My family invested a lot of sweat in that place. It was *their* place in the world, and now it's my place. Maybe some day I'll have kids and they won't want it, but fact is, I'm rooted here until I die."

"That must be a good feeling."

"Sometimes." He hesitated. "You?"

"Rootless. I have no way to really understand how you must feel about your ranch. My mom moved us around the country a lot. I was lucky to finish high school in the same town where I started it."

"And you've continued the gypsy tradition?"

"You mean because I came here?"

"For one. But what about the past?"

"I've moved a lot, too. You want the truth? It's getting old. I've never known anyone for more than a few years, and then they get left behind. I started thinking about that, and it struck me that's a really lonely way to live."

"So you're looking for a place to stay permanently?"

"If I can find one."

"Why this place?"

"Because it feels right. Because after I'd spent a week here considering the job, I got the feeling that if I stayed long enough to become a part of the community, I could put down some really deep roots. People wouldn't be strangers on a busy street. They'd have names, and I'd get to know them at least a bit. That maybe someday I wouldn't be an outsider anymore."

"So you've always been an outsider?"

"I've never been anything else."

He fell silent, pulling into a faculty parking spot near

the west wing door. From here she could see the freshly painted and repaired roof and side wall. "Someone said a tornado hit the building?"

"Yeah, last spring. What a mess, but at least no one was killed. It just grazed the town, but the thing was a half mile wide. If you get out into the countryside you can still see the scars where it passed. At least no one was killed, although we had some injuries."

"Is that common here? Tornadoes?"

"It's really rare. I won't say never, but what we saw last spring was one for the record books."

"Nobody told me how bad it was."

He gave her an amused glance as he turned off the ignition. "They probably didn't want to scare you away."

"I've lived in tornado country. It wouldn't panic me. I just prefer it if they're not common."

"They certainly aren't here."

As they climbed out and headed inside, she could hear sounds from the athletic fields on the other side of the building. "Practice today?"

"Not until later. I think some youngsters must be playing on the outdoor basketball courts." He unlocked the door and held it open for her.

"Why would the school have outdoor courts? I never got that."

"Only the team and supervised students get to play basketball in the gymnasium. Outdoors is for fun and practice."

"That's really a nice idea." But she couldn't help thinking he had brought her to this side of the school in case some of the basketball players were out there. Or some of the kids she had interrupted yesterday. She doubted he was afraid of any of them, so he must be trying to avoid giving her a moment of discomfort. A generous thought, but really not necessary. She liked to believe she was tougher than that.

They wended their way through virtually empty hallways. In the distance they could hear a janitor working with a buffer, but other than that the place seemed abandoned.

He took her to his office just off the gymnasium, not to his homeroom. She guessed it made sense that he'd have two offices given that he wore two hats at the school.

It wasn't a huge space, but it contained enough room for maybe half-a-dozen students to gather with him, and a counter where he had a coffeepot and microwave.

"This is positively homey," she tried to joke.

"Given their age, high metabolism and activity level, it takes a lot of effort to keep those young men fed. That microwave gets a megaworkout."

"I bet."

He cleared a stack of papers to one side, pulled a chair around so she could see his computer screen and turned on the machine.

"Okay," he said. "You've worked in a lot of different places. How familiar are you with antibullying programs? How much do you already know about the dangers of bullying?"

"Some," she admitted. "In one of the schools where I worked, the program had been in place for at least ten years. It started in kindergarten, actually, and was covered every single year."

"What were the important mechanisms?"

"First, faculty and administration. It's so important for teachers not to ignore bullying, to listen to student complaints about it and do something, and for the administration to be fully involved. You get nowhere if the adults in the school brush it off."

He nodded, his blue eyes touching lightly on her face before returning to the computer screen. She wondered, half-humorously, if he would have liked to dive into the monitor to escape. "And the students?"

"We tried to create a culture where bullying was frowned on. You know as well as I do that peer pressure is more important to youngsters than anything adults do or say. So if you can persuade the students to self-police, to look down on bullies, you can stop a lot of it."

"That's going to be the hard part."

"No kidding. Changing a culture takes time. One assembly won't do it, it'll just get the ball rolling. This is going to have to be an ongoing program."

"Where do you suggest we start?"

She liked that he was looking to her for advice. Even in this supposedly more equal time, she was used to men just taking over and directing projects. She'd always put it down to testosterone or something, but maybe it wasn't. Linc didn't strike her as short on testosterone or manliness, come to that.

"Ideally," she said slowly, "we'd like to get the cooperation of students who are looked up to. The tone-setters."

"Like some of my players."

"Exactly. They can be our first peer-pressure group, the guys and gals most of the other students respect."

"We need to get across how dangerous this really is. It's not just a matter of scaring or upsetting another student."

"No," she agreed. "It can have lifelong consequences. It can cause posttraumatic stress disorder. And have you looked at the rate of teen suicide? A lot of those can be linked directly to bullying."

"We've definitely got our work cut out for us. First to get the staff and a core of students on our side. Once we have the kernels we'll need to help them grow."

Then he looked at her. "Have you ever been bullied?"

"Of course. Most people have been."

"Badly?"

She hesitated then sighed. "I guess. I got picked on a lot for my weight."

He astonished her then. "I don't see anything wrong with your weight. Were you heavier back then?"

"Actually, not by much."

He shook his head. "Amazing. I would have thought most men would have thought you were gorgeous."

Her jaw dropped but he had already turned away. "I wondered," he said, returning to the subject at hand, "because you didn't seem to take the way those guys brushed against you as bullying. Almost as if it were normal."

"I didn't think of it that way," she admitted. "It was a little strong but I didn't feel intimidated."

Blue eyes settled on her again. "Really? But that's what they intended, don't you think? Letting you know that they were bigger and stronger and not afraid to push?"

She bit her lip, considering it. "I guess so. There was no other reason for it. They didn't frighten me, though. I just got angrier."

"Somebody sure tried to frighten you this morning." He frowned then and leaned back a bit in his chair, as if thinking things over. "I don't like this," he said. "Bullying in general, of course, but I don't like the way it seems to have escalated, judging by what you saw and what you experienced. Some element is getting way out of line and we need to yank them back as quickly as possible."

"Maybe it's just the four I caught in the act. Maybe it isn't a trend at all."

One corner of his mouth tipped up, and his eyes scraped over her briefly. "You're quite the optimist. I'm more inclined to think this is the tip of the iceberg. These things don't usually happen in total isolation."

She rested her chin on her hand. "You might be right."

"I hope I'm not," he admitted. "Unfortunately, I've been watching that steady fracturing I mentioned yesterday ever since the semiconductor plant arrived. Little by little a line has been drawn. And when you start drawing lines, how long is it before the people on the other side of the line from you become objects of your scorn?"

"You may be right."

"Basic social dynamics. We've always gone to war over our differences. A school is just a microcosm." He shook his head. "Don't let me start thinking about humanity as a whole. Right now we need to deal with a front-and-center neighborhood problem with as little scarring and fallout as possible."

She gave a laugh. "Yeah, we can't reform humanity in a day, or a school in even a week. How do you want to approach this?"

He took the task of finding the students for his core peer group, and she agreed to set about finding materials that they could use in a more public venue.

Then he rose, stretched and said, "I've got a team meeting in a little while. I'll drive you home."

"I prefer to walk, but thanks."

"Then I'll walk with you."

His words stilled her. "You really *are* worried about that call."

"I wouldn't say I'm worried, but a little caution might be wise until we see if you get harassed again."

She felt an instant of rebellion. She was an independent woman who felt perfectly capable of taking care of herself, and she didn't need a white knight to protect her. On the other hand, it would mean a little extra time with him, which she wouldn't mind. Maybe she could get past the force field a little.

Pulling on her jacket, she remarked, "I thought this was a friendly, nice county."

"It is, mostly. But like any other place on the planet, not everyone is nice."

Outside, the air still had that wonderful crisp feel of fall, and she almost thought she could smell snow in the air even though the sun was bright. After he locked the door, they began to stroll toward her house, carrying the travel mugs. He didn't seem to be in a hurry.

"How do you like living here so far?" he asked.

"I'm loving it, actually."

"Not dying for lack of nightclubs, theaters and huge shopping malls?"

She laughed. "Not at all. I've never enjoyed mall-crawling, for one thing. I'm always looking for little out-of-the way places full of different things."

"We have plenty of those."

"I've noticed. It's one of the things that charmed me. I haven't been in a department store like Freitag's since I was a little kid. I get a kick out of having the wood floors creak under my feet. Besides, if you've seen one mall, you've pretty much seen them all. The homogenization of America. You can't tell what city you're in."

"That's my impression. But what about things to do?"

"There's plenty to do." She glanced at him, wondering

about the line of questioning. "I get together with some teachers to play cards a couple of times a month. We go out for lunch and sometimes dinner. I never liked the club scene. I guess most people would find me dull."

"Not around here."

"And if I ever get an overwhelming urge for a museum or the theater, I can take a weekend and go to Denver. Come on, Linc. You teach. You know how little free time you have."

He chuckled. "You're right. And there's even less with my ranch."

"And football," she reminded him. "Anyway, I really like it here so far. It's different from the places I lived before, but I'm finding it comfortable."

"I'll ask for your opinion again come early March."

She was laughing when he left her at her door, but his smile was faint, and she could almost hear the shield cranking back into place.

What was it with that man?

Sighing, she went inside, taking his advice to lock up behind herself, and decided she would probably never know.

Whatever his problem, Linc had clearly decided not to let her into his circle.

To hell with him, she thought, returning to work on her week's plans. She needed an idea to excite her students more than she needed him.

# *Chapter 3*

Sunday night turned wildly windy and Cassie awoke to a Monday morning with steel-gray skies and air that felt surprisingly warm. The wind had taken the last of the leaves from the trees, and was still blowing them around as she walked to the school.

With no more phone calls, she felt the incident was closed. Over the weekend, though, she'd been texted by Les, the principal, asking that she and Linc speak to the faculty at the weekly meeting at the close of school that day.

Being the new kid on the block, as it were, she didn't feel entirely comfortable with that idea, and as she walked she realized she had a minor case of nerves going, the way she often did on the very first day of the school year. Great. She hoped she'd forget about it during the teaching day.

When she reached the school, she found Linc was still on bus duty. At least he smiled faintly when he opened the door for her.

"About this afternoon…" she began.

He nodded. "I can do most of the talking. I understand you don't want to come off like the new broom."

"Exactly. Thank you."

Another brief nod. "You just fill in when you think I've left something out. I managed to get some of the first few members of our student squad, though. Some of my star players and a handful of the cheerleaders. I didn't make a general approach, just handpicked a few, but no turn-downs."

She turned as she stepped inside. "That's fabulous!"

He grinned, surprising her. "Despite what happened on Friday, most of our students are good people."

She smiled as she walked to her classroom, thinking it was a good start and they'd probably get a handle on the bullying before there was too much more of it. Maybe James Carney and others like him wouldn't have to endure as much.

She unlocked the door of her classroom and stepped inside. Immediately she smelled something awful, something sickeningly sweet. Going to her desk, what she saw made her gasp in horror and back up to the door, where she hit the intercom button.

"School office."

"Marian, I need Les right now. Someone left a dead rat on my desk and I'm not going to be able to let the students in."

She heard Marian talk to someone. "He'll be right there with the janitor."

She stepped outside and locked her door again, standing guard, trying to keep her breakfast down. Ugly. Ugly. The thing had had its throat cut, there was blood all over her desk pad, and from the odor it had been left to rot all weekend.

The message was unmistakable, and almost enough to make her double over and heave. She could feel a cold sweat breaking out all over her body, and the nausea was overwhelming. She wanted to leave and never come back.

She kept drawing deep breaths to steady herself, leaning against the wall for support, and telling herself not to be hysterical. It was a nasty, messy, ugly message, but that's all it was.

If they wanted to frighten her off, it wasn't going to work. She promised herself that even as she felt the urge to leave and not come back. How would she ever sit at that desk again without remembering that rat?

She hated to think what kind of a person would have done that. One of those bullies? God, if it had been one of them, then James Carney could be in serious trouble.

For that matter, so could she.

Several students arrived before Les. "Sorry," she told them, "you'll have to wait in the library or lunch room. There's a bit of a mess that needs cleaning."

Did she imagine it, or did one of the boys actually smirk? Anything was possible, but she told herself not to see everyone as a potential enemy in this. She was likely being hypersensitive.

The nausea had mostly passed by the time Les arrived with the janitor on his heels. Amazingly, Linc wasn't far behind.

Les eyed her critically. "How bad is it?"

"Bad enough that I'm sending my homeroom to the library or cafeteria. Someone is going to have to take attendance. It's a mess."

"Well, let's see it."

She turned to unlock the door. "You'll excuse me if I don't go in there again."

Linc went in, though, and she noticed he took out his cell phone and snapped a few photos. Les gagged. The janitor even paled, and he must have cleaned up some real messes during his tenure.

"This goes way beyond a prank," Linc said flatly. "I think we need to call the sheriff."

Les nodded, putting his hand over his mouth and hurrying toward the door. "Don't touch it. I'll get Gage out here."

"I need to hold class," Cassie said, trying to cling to some semblance of normalcy or routine. Focusing on the one thing she *could* do.

"I'll arrange for a blackboard in the cafeteria," Les said as he hurried up the hall. "And I'll call the sheriff."

The janitor, a guy who preferred to be called Gus even though his name was Madson Carson, just stood there shaking his head. "What's the world coming to?" he asked. "Who the hell got in here?"

"It's been here at least since Friday," Linc remarked. "Let's get out and wait for the sheriff. I doubt he'll find anything useful, but we don't want to contaminate it."

Once the door was locked again, he drew Cassie to one side, holding her elbow gently. "Are you okay?"

"I will be. How could somebody get in to do that?"

"Remember, you can always get out of the building. All someone had to do was lay in wait until the place was empty."

It was true, she realized. All the doors were fire doors, and would open from the inside even when locked. As for her classroom…master keys could be had from several places. Or the lock could be picked easily enough. It wasn't exactly a vault.

She bent and looked at the keyhole. "Someone picked it," she said as she saw some deformation around the lock.

"Maybe." Linc sighed. "Damn, what's happening around here?"

She had no answers. Straightening, she looked at him. "Reality. Like you said, every place has its bad apples."

The hall was becoming crowded with students, and the PA system burst into life, announcing that Ms. Greaves's classes would be held in the cafeteria today.

"It bothers me how fast this had to have happened," Linc said. "The incident was Friday at noon. It's possible that when I opened the school to let the team in someone snuck in with them, but that's still the same day as the bullying, and probably a short time after Les called parents."

"How many people were in here Friday night?"

"The boosters, the team, some other parents, a few teachers. The cheerleaders. There's always a crowd before we leave for an away game."

"In short, too many suspects."

He nodded, but frowned at the same time. "Are you sure you're going to be all right? You could take a sick day."

"And spend all day at home thinking about this?" She shook her head. "No, thanks. What's that they say about after you fall from a horse?"

His frown turned to a faint smile. "You've got some backbone. Okay. But depending on how much of a threat the sheriff thinks this is, maybe you should take care not to be alone."

As if she would have a choice.

The sheriff arrived with his crime scene unit, and Cassie was grateful that the students had all vanished into classrooms. Not that they wouldn't hear about this, not that word wouldn't get out, but they didn't need to be clustered around and hearing gory details, or getting in the way.

The sheriff, Gage Dalton, whom she'd met a couple of times before casually, was gentle and kind with his questioning of her. He started with that morning, but inevitably he worked back to the possible motivation for this treatment.

She looked at Les, who sighed and nodded. "We may as well talk about it all, even though we're going to do our part, perhaps the most important part. You do have plans?"

"We're working on them. Linc and I have both started."

"With what?" Gage asked.

So she explained the bullying incident. Linc refused to let her skip over the phone call she had received. When they fell silent, having explained their plans for dealing with bullying, Gage's face was dark.

"So," he said, looking at Les, "you thought it was a good idea to hang your teacher out on this?" He turned to Linc. "What about you?"

Cassie spoke first. "Our main concern was not to get James Carney into more trouble. We were trying to protect him."

"So you get blamed for the detentions? You become the focus of this gang?"

"I don't like it," Linc said bluntly. "In fact, it concerns me a whole lot, and more now than it did on Friday. The fact remains, the Carney boy wasn't the only one bullied. Cassie was bullied, too. So it seemed we needed to deal with that immediately, without getting Carney into more trouble. We can't have students making implied threats by pushing teachers and ignoring them or we'll have anarchy, and we won't be able to control anything."

Gage hitched his gun belt, grimaced a bit and leaned

against the wall. "You know I could make arrests for what happened Friday. I get the part about not wanting to ruin a young person's life. I completely get it and don't want to do that. But given that you had warning of violence, however mild, this is one bull you should have taken by the horns immediately."

"James Carney…" Cassie began.

"I get it about the Carney kid. Believe me, I get it. But despite these moves against Cassie, are you really sure you've deflected the attention from him? I doubt it. They're going to know what's behind this. All you've done is give them a second object." He shook his head. "Too many suspects now, too. The bullies, their parents, their friends… Unless we find some specific evidence in that mess on Cassie's desk, we're going to be stymied. So keep that in mind. This has escalated. Keep that in mind, too."

Linc walked Cassie to the cafeteria and she got the feeling she wasn't the only unhappy one.

"We were stupid," he announced.

"I don't think so. Les was right about dealing with the infraction against me and leaving James out of it for now."

He looked at her, brows lifted. "You can say that after this morning?"

She bit her lip, then nodded. As nerve-racking as this had become, she didn't want to do anything to give those bullies more fuel against James. "I can protect myself," she said stoutly.

He took her elbow and drew her into a deserted spur of hallway that led to the janitorial rooms. "Don't underestimate this, Cassie. That rat this morning…that's extreme. You'd already been bullied twice. This goes a little beyond that, don't you think?"

She looked up at him and found his gaze steady and

concerned. For once he wasn't trying to look at something else. The impact of his full attention nearly left her breathless. How could he have that effect with a mere look?

She had to gather suddenly scattered thoughts, and that involved dropping her own gaze briefly. "I'm older," she said. "I'm an adult. I can handle it better."

"Even a rotting bloody rat on your desk? Are you so sure, Cassie?"

"Students are different here. Hunting is a part of life for them. This probably doesn't strike them the same way it would if a suburban student were to think of such a thing."

"Now you're making excuses."

"Am I wrong?"

"I don't know," he said forcefully. "And that's what's bothering me. Yes, hunting is a part of life for most of our students, but it isn't usually sport, and it certainly isn't done for reasons of cruelty. A lot of families look forward to deer or elk to get them through the winter. Killing for the sake of killing isn't approved by most folks."

"And rats are vermin to be exterminated," she argued, though he was beginning to make her stomach twist edgily again. Maybe there was no way at all to minimize this. Maybe she shouldn't even try. But she didn't want to walk around the halls of her new school looking on every student as a potential threat. Heck, she liked almost all of her students.

"Cassie," he said quietly, "don't be stubborn. You know this was an awful thing to do to you *and* that rat."

Some bit of her ego deflated. Her hands came together, clasping tightly. "I know," she admitted quietly. "But I've got to get through the day, Linc. I've got to teach, and I have to like my students insofar as humanly possible. I can't let this poison my relationship with them."

He sighed, then nodded. "You're right. I just want you to stay alert, okay? Keep an eye out. Pay attention. Don't go blithely on as if nothing happened until we get this sorted out."

"Blithe is not my reaction to this," she said a little tartly. "Far from it. I wish I could scrub that image from my brain."

"I'm sure you do." He astonished her by reaching out to give her shoulder a squeeze. "Do me a favor. Let me see you home after the meeting this afternoon. Do it for me. I'll feel better."

For a guy who had been avoiding her like the plague, he was getting close awfully fast. He must have a wide streak of white knight in him, she thought. "Okay, thanks," she said finally. It wouldn't hurt and at this point she wasn't exactly as full of confidence as she was trying to project.

But after all her wishing that he wouldn't remain so distant, she wished something nicer had brought them together.

With that gloomy thought, she headed down the nearly deserted hallway to take over her first class of the day, a class that was almost over. So much for great ideas. She'd have to bring them up to speed tomorrow.

She could also tell by some of the looks and whispers as she approached the group in the cafeteria that word had already gotten around. She wondered if they had the details or were going to question her about it all. Twenty-two pairs of eyes fixed on her, but no one said a word.

"Well, it looks like you guys lucked out," she said brightly. "Since I don't have time to cover new material, there will be no math problems for homework. And as for the project for the week, this is your turn to come up with one you'd like using the math and science we cover in class. I want to hear your ideas tomorrow."

At least they seemed eager about coming up with their own projects. By the time they headed out a few minutes later, many were already talking about ideas.

The rest of the day held nothing unusual until she received word that her classroom was once again ready for her. She'd have liked to avoid it at least until tomorrow, but shortly after she was informed, the public address system announced the rest of her classes would be held in the regular classroom.

Damn, she thought, torn between amusement and distaste, which was an odd place to be. She gathered up her materials into her book bag and set out with the migrating students. Gus was waiting for her.

"I got it all cleaned up," he told her. "All of it. Sorry, had to throw out a few things. The school will replace them."

"Thank you, Gus. I'm sorry you had to deal with that."

"I clean up messes all the time, but never one that made me so mad. Don't choke on the air freshener, but that smell didn't want to quit."

She sniffed the air. "You did a good job."

He smiled awkwardly. "You need anything at all, just let me know."

Another white knight, she thought. "Can I be honest? I hope I don't need you again for anything like this."

He laughed and headed out as students began pouring through the door.

In all, the day felt fractured, everything off-kilter, and she was sure she didn't do the best job of teaching. She wound up giving all her students a night off from homework because she wasn't sure she had really explained anything clearly enough. They seemed to be happy about coming up with their own projects, however, and she found herself anticipating hearing their ideas. So at least something good had happened that day.

The faculty meeting after school disturbed her, too. She was tired to begin with, probably because the day had been emotionally stressful, but to get in there and find there were teachers who didn't believe the bullying needed to be addressed left her both astonished and disappointed.

There were a significant number who felt the incident with James Carney was so unusual that it didn't really mean anything. Others felt that kids were just being kids. She was relieved, however, to find that more than half the teachers agreed bullying needed to be addressed firmly and quickly.

She was so glad Linc did most of the talking. Within ten minutes she realized that if she had tried to present the problem and the plans, she would have been dismissed. She was an outsider who knew nothing about their school or their students, and she would have been marked as being hypercritical about things she didn't understand.

Linc's presentation was at least received with respect, if not a hugely warm reception from everyone.

"They don't want to believe it's going on," she said to Linc as he walked her home. "Is it really that invisible?"

"My guess is yes. The students don't engage in that kind of behavior around teachers. At least not when they get to this age. Maybe that's why we thought it was tapering off after middle school. You heard what I said Friday to Les. We usually don't see this kind of extreme bullying at this age. Obviously, that doesn't mean it doesn't happen."

"Obviously." She sighed. "And maybe this really was an isolated incident. But I don't like the way it seems to be snowballing."

"Me, either. I'm really sorry about this morning. That must have given you a distaste for this place."

"Actually, no," she answered truthfully. "There was a while this morning when I didn't want to be in school. I admit it. The hardest part turned out to be trying not to be suspicious of every student in my classes. I like most of them. I don't think any of them were involved, but it still felt like I was attending a lineup for a few hours there."

He cracked a laugh. "I have no trouble imagining that. But you got past it?"

"Of course. It was temporary. The thing is, Linc, I've been teaching for a few years. Bad things happen, students do stupid and ugly things sometimes. It's all a part of growing up. It's not like I'm going to judge this entire county by one incident."

She felt him glance over at her, but she kept her gaze fixed on the street ahead. He might be stepping in right now out of a concern for her, but she had already realized he wasn't interested in any more than that.

"So you're not going to quit and leave?"

That startled her. She looked at him then. "It hadn't crossed my mind. Should it?"

"I hope not. I hear good things about your teaching. Your students mostly don't hate math, which is something approaching a miracle to my way of thinking."

She laughed. "We'll see what happens as the year goes on."

"I suppose we will."

They had reached her door. She had planned to invite him in for a coffee or a snack, but something in the way he said that caused her to pause and face him. "What is it?" she asked him. "You keep saying things that sound like you expect me to leave, or fall flat on my face. Did I do something?"

His face froze for an instant. "No," he said finally. "Most people who didn't grow up here don't like living here for long. Hell, some who *did* grow up here can't wait to leave."

She tilted her head, studying him. "Then I guess we *will* have to see, won't we?"

"That's all I'm saying. Keep your doors locked and don't hesitate to call the sheriff if anything worries you. It's been my experience he'd rather be called over nothing than not be called when he's really needed."

She nodded.

"We'll get through to the holdouts on the bullying," he said firmly. "It may take a little time, but not much. With one or two notable exceptions, the faculty here are primarily interested in student welfare."

She nodded, hoping he was right. "Coffee or a snack?"

He shook his head. "I've got to get back to practice. See you tomorrow."

The shields had slammed back into place, the conversation firmly on business again. Perplexed, she went inside, locked the door and watched him walk away back toward the school. The wind was picking up again, and leaves swirled around the sidewalk and streets.

He looked lonely, she thought, as he strode away into the gray afternoon. But maybe she was imagining that because he seemed determined to keep a distance between them.

One minute approachable, the next as far away as the moon. He was going to drive her nuts with that. Not worth it, she told herself. Maybe he was the most attractive man she'd ever met, but attraction was meaningless without a lot of other important stuff, stuff which he clearly didn't intend to offer.

She needed to think about other things, and quit letting her hormones get the better of her. It was one big waste of time, and she had more important matters to spend energy on.

Like class planning, upcoming parent-teacher conferences and the bullying program.

Then it struck her she hadn't seen James around the school today. Not even in class. How could she have missed that?

Because of a butchered rat on her desk and all the ensuing dislocation. Frowning, she pulled out her class roster, shoved the disk into her computer and called up James's name and phone number. It wouldn't hurt to find out if he was sick. For the moment she refused to consider other possibilities.

James answered the phone on the first ring. "I'm fine," he said, almost truculently. "Just fine. I felt sick this morning is all."

"Will you be in tomorrow?"

"Probably. It's okay, Ms. Greaves. Stop worrying about me."

But as she hung up, Cassie was even more worried than before.

Practice kept Linc pretty well preoccupied until he finally closed up the gym around six-thirty. He needed to get back to his animals, but it was as if the instant he stopped thinking about his team, all he could think about was Cassie. That was so not good on a bunch of levels.

He got in his truck, fully intending to ignore all other

impulses and head home. Instead his truck took charge and he found himself parked in front of Cassie's place.

Hell, he thought, rapping his fingers on the steering wheel. Then with a sigh, he gave up the battle. Climbing out, he walked up to her door and rang the bell. He was glad to see that she peeked out the side window before opening the door. While such measures were rarely needed around here, given that phone call and the rat, a little caution seemed in order.

"Linc!" she said in surprise as she opened the door. "Is something wrong?"

"Not a thing." Boy, this was going to sound stupid. "I just had a wild idea and wondered if you'd like to come out to my ranch with me. You can help me feed animals and see a different part of life around here. Unless you're too busy."

Delight chased surprise across her face. "I'd really, truly like that."

"I can get you home in plenty of time," he offered reassuringly. And maybe if she saw what the rest of his life was like, she'd stop looking at him with those unmistakable flickers of longing, flickers that were definitely getting under his skin. He tried to tell himself it was just because he was a man who hadn't been with a woman in a long time, but that didn't seem to be working.

So he'd give *her* the cold shower, the one he called the rest of his life. He could only listen to his own reasoning with amusement, wondering if he were engaging in a little self-deception, or really so sure this would work.

No, of course it wouldn't work. It had taken Martha more than a year to get totally fed up. On the other hand, Cassie struck him as being a whole lot more honest in her reactions than Martha. Sometimes he looked back at his engagement and wondered if Martha had believed from the outset that he'd sell the ranch, move and support them in a more comfortable lifestyle, one she seemed to want.

The thought now almost made him laugh. Like you could sell a small ranch these days. It wasn't as if there were enough around here to make some wealthy guy from the city want to plant himself here, even for a summer home, unless all he wanted to do was ride horses until he dropped and maybe hunt in the autumn.

He'd seen other places like his sell, but these days they were usually part of a larger buyout of a group of ranches, usually for industrial farming, or subdivisions. No subdivisions likely to be built around here in the foreseeable future, and he doubted many, if any, of his neighbors would want to sell. Most of them, like him, seemed firmly rooted in Conard County.

Regardless, he wouldn't put a dollar value on his way of life, and he wouldn't give up his legacy.

Cassie spoke as they headed out of town. "The shortening of the days is more obvious here than when I lived down south."

"I imagine it would be." It was an innocuous line of conversation, covering a topic they both knew.

"I'd forgotten," she said. "You get used to the difference in latitude quickly and don't even think about it. By next spring I probably won't even notice anymore."

"It's not as remarkable here as some places even farther north. Funny story. I was visiting a friend up in Canada one summer and I couldn't figure out why I was waking up so late every morning. I mean, the day was dang near half-gone. My friend laughed and suggested I look at the time I was going to bed. I was running by the sun and it amazed me to realize a couple of hours after sunset up there was the wee hours of the morning. I was getting to bed around 2:00 a.m. without even realizing it."

She laughed. "I'm not sure I could handle it up around the Arctic Circle. The long days would be one thing, but I think the endless nights might be too much."

"They are even for some folks who grow up there."

She fell silent then, appearing content to look out at the darkening countryside as they passed. A while later she remarked on all the tumbleweed caught in fences. "I had no idea it could get that big."

"Most of the time it gets hung up somewhere on the fences, but if the wind gets really stiff, look out. It can blow loose and be a driving hazard."

"So you have goats and sheep?"

"Yeah. And a few horses."

"Is your ranch a going concern? Or just something you do in addition to teaching?"

He thought about that a bit before answering because it wasn't something he had really settled with himself. "I like teaching. I like coaching football. But I also like working around the ranch. I guess I'm fortunate my spread isn't big enough to really make it full-time. Once it would have been, but not now. Economics have changed for small ranches."

"That's sad."

He shrugged. "The world changes. I get variety in exchange."

He glanced over and saw she had twisted in her seat to look at him. "But if you could make it full-time…?"

"I don't know. I'd have to get some additional land, or find some grazing to lease. Some of my neighbors lease out their land. Others lease it from them. And of course, there are grazing rights I could get on public lands. The thing is, unless you're a really big operation these days, it doesn't take much to break you. So it's best to just do it this way."

"A lot of people don't know it, but not so long ago Florida was the second largest cattle producer in the country."

"So you saw a lot of ranches?"

"Huge ones. Then we had a really bad drought. Maybe you remember it. We had to import hay and feed from all over the country. I never saw so many skinny cattle in my life. Bones sticking out. Water was so scarce the alligators were on the move looking for any pond they could find and sadly many didn't make it. Anyway, after that a lot of the ranches in my area started selling off large parcels for subdivisions and shopping centers. It kind of felt like it was one straw too many for some of our biggest ranches."

He shook his head. "There are advantages to staying small. At least I know I can get through those times. The big guys get into serious trouble fast. I'm sorry."

"It was sad," she agreed. "A whole way of life started vanishing. I can only imagine how hard it was on those families. At least some of them had a way out."

He felt a pang of sympathy for those ranchers. How could he not? But he wanted to keep the conversation cheerful. "Did I just hear you offer sympathy to gators?"

A laugh escaped her, a pleasant, happy sound. "You bet. It's possible to coexist with them, you know. And they were there before we moved in on them. All you have to do is treat nature with respect."

"So I take it you'd advocate for wolves."

"I would. How about you?"

"I'm all for it. They improve the ecosystem. Sure, I lose the occasional lamb or kid, but I was losing them to coyotes long before the wolves were reintroduced."

"How do your protect your herds?"

"Dogs. Big, great, wonderful, furry dogs. Bears hate 'em, wolves avoid them and coyotes run like hell. Be prepared to get jumped on and licked to death. Other than charging them with taking care of the sheep and goats, I pretty much just let 'em be dogs."

She laughed again. "I like that."

Martha sure hadn't. Her idea of a dog was something that could sit on her lap, smell like perfume and wear a bow. She really hadn't been able to handle his dusty, dirty, grubby working dogs

Well, he'd see how this one reacted soon enough.

It was nearly dark by the time they reached the ranch. Cloud cover eliminated any light at all, so he asked Cassie to remain in the truck while he turned on the security lights. He used them only when it couldn't be avoided and he hated to think about the energy they burned since they were essentially floodlights, much brighter than streetlights.

But they had the predictable effect. As soon as they flipped on, sheep and goats began to hurry toward the fence looking for the additional feed he gave them, and the dogs, who had started waiting joyously probably long before he even reached his driveway, were barking wildly. They knew he'd give them treats after their hard work, chewy stuff that tasted like bacon and turkey, which they gobbled down before even going for their kibble.

The horses were calmer, coming to the pasture fence at a more sedate pace. Of course, they'd probably done a lot more running during the day than the sheep or goats.

He heard Cassie crunch across autumn-dry grass toward him as he watched the gathering.

"You have more animals than I thought," she remarked. "Are goats friendly?"

"A goat would move in with you if she could. At least these would. They come closer to being pets than the sheep, actually."

"How neat! What can I do to help?"

That was a question Martha hadn't asked, not the first time. In fact, come to think of it, he couldn't remember her ever offering to help without being asked.

Cassie, on the other hand, dove right in, seeming glad to do everything he asked. And when she went to feed the dogs for him, the six big gangbusters managed to knock her to the ground in their eagerness. Kibble flew everywhere. She sat on her butt, looking astonished, and he started to race toward her, but then she laughed and accepted all the gentle butting and didn't even complain when she got her face licked.

No, she dug her hands into dusty fur and scratched every animal she could reach. They approved, clearly, and ignored him for the moment.

"A love affair begins," he drawled, leaning against the fence post.

She grinned up at him. "But I spilled their food. How will they eat? Do I need to get more?"

"They'll find it. That's what they have noses for." He pulled a bag of treats out of his pocket and tossed it to her. She caught it. "One each."

The dogs knew what was coming. They swarmed her anew, and her laughter filled the night. He could feel his own face stretching into a grin. He hadn't expected this at all. Not for one second.

She struggled to her feet before opening the treat bag. There was one bit of manners Linc insisted on, and he said,

"Tell them to sit before you give them treats. Just hold out your hand palm down and say *sit*."

She followed his direction and instantly had six dogs sitting facing her. They jostled each other a bit, but kept their butts on the ground.

She giggled again.

"Don't let them snap it from you. If one of them tries just say 'no' sharply."

Barking had turned to impatient whines, but much to his relief they behaved perfectly. They were big dogs, part herders and part other breeds, certainly one that wasn't afraid of bears. He had no idea anymore. These dogs had all descended from the first dogs on the ranch and whatever else they'd mated with over the years. Letting the dogs pretty much have free rein outdoors meant that litters were often indeterminate. There might even be some wolf in there now among the younger dogs for all he knew. He even suspected some coyote. He kept the population down, though, by neutering all but one breeding pair. As it was, he still had plenty of requests for puppies from other ranchers.

"They're good dogs," he remarked. "They do most of the hard work for me."

"The best helpers in the world, I imagine."

She petted them some more, seeming almost reluctant to leave them, but when he moved on to tend to the sheep and goats, she followed along and helped. She appeared enchanted by both, never made a complaint about them being smelly, and then was delighted when she was able to help him stable the three horses.

"Horses are so beautiful," she remarked while he checked hooves then gave them all fresh hay and a little bit of oats. "Do you ride often?"

"As often as time allows. Not so much in the fall, what with football."

"I've only ridden once, when I was little kid, and was led around by a bridle."

"We'll have to do something about that." As soon as the words popped out, he could almost see them written in the air. What the hell was he thinking? He'd brought her out here to turn her off, not offer to see her again.

Instead she'd shattered all his preconceptions about her, and now he was offering to take her riding? He considered banging his head on a stall post to get his brain back into working order.

Too late. Well, he reassured himself, he was busy with football, and they had this whole bullying thing to deal with. He could reasonably avoid having time to take her riding until spring. And by then, she'd probably be crying uncle about this whole middle-of-nowhere place, and pining to have a bagel shop around the corner or something.

The nights were growing chilly enough that he blanketed the horses because they couldn't move much to keep warm. On the coldest nights he could blow heat into this barn, but like everything else, he did his best to conserve by avoiding it as much as possible.

He should have taken her home then, but he didn't like to be needlessly rude, even to protect himself. Instead, he invited her in for a hot drink and light snack. She might as well see the rest of it, the farmhouse that had seen better days, the furnishings left over from earlier generations. There was a difference between maintenance and decorating, and while he was good at the former, he had little interest in the latter. And, frankly, little enough money to

waste on nonessentials. Or maybe that was largely his preference. If it served its purpose, it was good enough for him.

The kitchen was an old farmhouse kitchen, huge enough
to feed the hands when necessary. The days when this
place had been able to hire hands were past, but the kitchen
and its long trestle table remained, as did the huge mudroom leading into it.

If he let himself think about it, he could hear better
times almost whispering around him. Better times for the
ranch, that was. He certainly didn't think his own times
were bad.

Cassie stood on the threshold blinking. "Did you guys
build for an army?"

He had to laugh as he motioned her to the table. "Families were a lot bigger in the old days. And back then we
had hired hands to feed, too."

She sat, watching him as he moved around making
some hot chocolate and breaking out some cookies. "What
changed, Linc?"

"The times. After the Second World War, everybody
but my grandfather moved away. The G.I. Bill helped with
that, I guess. Regardless, my great-grandfather also broke
up the land, so his kids could have a share. From the stories I hear, it didn't make much difference because everyone was working together anyway. But after the war…" He
shrugged. "My granddad bought them back as everyone
started moving away. We've still got a few thousand acres
but the economics of things now make them almost pointless to put into use. You could call it splendid isolation."

A smile flickered over her features as he turned toward
her to put the cookies on the table, but his face looked almost sad. "How do you feel about that?" she asked.

"I'm okay with it. I keep my hand in, I sell wool, I sell lambs, and keep it to a level I can manage."

"Do you ever see it changing?"

He poured the cocoa from the pan into two mugs. "Not anytime soon."

She grew thoughtful and quiet, and he let her be as he joined her to sip his beverage and eat a store-bought cookie.

"It's funny," she said after a while. "Some things are growing rapidly, and other things are shrinking."

"Times change, needs change. Cultures move on."

"I know, but I'm not sure that's always good."

"Right now it's good for the land out there. I didn't just happen into biology by accident. I get a kick out of watching nature move back in."

"Your own little eco-sanctuary?"

He had to smile. "I guess so."

The thermostat had kicked on a little while ago, raising the house from its daytime setting of sixty to a more comfortable sixty-eight for the evening. As the room warmed, he began to detect Cassie's scents—aromas of laundry soap, shampoo and woman. Most especially woman. It was faint, but as it hit him, he knew he'd better get her home soon.

Then she tugged her jacket off and he got a whiff that filled him with an instant longing so strong his jeans felt tight. Not good. Had he been crazy? Had he really thought that bringing her out here to see the reality of his life would cause *her* to put up a wall between them?

Because she wasn't acting as if it had. She had honestly seemed to enjoy it all. Maybe that was its newness, but it certainly hadn't worked for turning her away yet.

Instead he would now have the powerful memory of

her sitting in his kitchen and smelling like temptation personified.

Yep, he'd been an idiot.

But there was no denying he liked having her here. Liked seeing another face across the table, liked the scents of woman that wafted around him. Liked not being alone.

Even though alone was where he was going to wind up. She'd never stay. Never. She might as well be trying life out on Mars.

Something indefinable flickered across her face, yet it communicated some kind of unhappiness. For all he'd avoided looking at her since she started teaching, he couldn't seem to stop looking now. Oh, he had it bad.

"I can't stop thinking of that rat," she said quietly.

That was nearly as good as an icy shower. He found it possible to breathe again and relax a little. "It was pretty bad," he admitted.

"Serial killers do things like that."

"So do stupid kids who routinely kill vermin and hunt."

Her green eyes looked almost haunted. "Seriously? Or are you just trying to reassure me?"

"You can't grow up on a ranch or farm around here without having killed things. It's just life. You shoot coyotes, you kill rats, you even have to butcher deer or elk or some steer that you raised from babyhood. It's a part of life, not a thrill."

"I guess I'm having trouble connecting with that."

"I can understand that. But you said it yourself earlier. You're from a different way of life. I'm just saying that these students are familiar with this kind of thing. It's part of protecting their ranches and feeding their families. No thrill in it, but they'd sure be able to guess it might give *you* the willies."

"Because I'm an outsider."

"Because you weren't ranch-raised. Kids in town find it repulsive, too, which makes them the butt of jokes sometimes. But killing a rat? That's nothing. They kill them all the time to keep them out of feed and out of the barns. I would almost bet the sheriff finds this one was caught in a trap before they killed it. And once it was in a trap, killing it would have been a mercy. Chances are it had a broken neck or back."

She shuddered. Well, he told himself, that was the reaction he had wanted. Too bad that he hated to see it.

"Okay," she said, appearing to stiffen herself. "I get it. I've trapped mice in my home upon occasion."

"Same thing. You're lucky if the trap kills them cleanly, but it doesn't always. And most folks around here don't want to put out poison for them."

"That's odd, because I've heard of poison bait being used to get rid of coyotes."

"It's allowed, but it's dangerous. Your dogs might get it. Your cats. And when it comes to rat poison, the problem gets bigger. So most of us try to avoid those methods. Cats and traps in the barn are preferred."

"I guess I've got a lot to learn."

He tried to smile reassuringly. "Everyone does. Look, I'm not defending what that culprit did, putting that rat on your desk. But while it was intended to upset you, and maybe frighten you, I doubt anyone meant it as a serious threat. Chances are some numskull thought it would be funny."

"God!" Worse was that she had taken this very sensible attitude only this morning, and now she was resisting the very reasoning she had offered herself. Why were her thoughts shifting like quicksand? Maybe she had felt braver at school, but the prospect of being home alone at night now didn't seem quite so safe. Harder to be above it all.

"There's no explaining the humor of a teen."

She knew he was right: the grosser, the better. They'd certainly achieved a total gross-out for her. "Then maybe we shouldn't have called the sheriff."

"Why? It may have been just an ugly prank but it remains it was vandalism and possibly another attempt to bully you. Having the sheriff investigate may have put an appropriate fear in certain people. There comes a point, Cassie, when you've got to realize that stuff you got away with as a child is no longer acceptable or even legal."

He paused, realizing he must seem to be going around in circles. Well, he probably was, between her damned scent and his own uncertainty about what was happening.

"I'll be honest with you," he said slowly. "I'm not really sure what's going on here. I'm wondering what's been bubbling beneath the surface at the school that I'm not aware of. That makes me uneasy. Obviously, something has been getting out of control. On the one hand, I'm trying to paint it in the best light because I know these kids. Or thought I did. I don't want to think the worst of any of them. On the other hand, I guess I shouldn't minimize it. There have been three transgressions we know about with you. Four if we add James. I'm not going to dismiss it, but I'm not going to be Chicken Little yet, either. The mind of a teenage male is impenetrable."

She surprised him by losing her haunted look and actually laughing. "You're right, it is. And girls aren't much better at that age."

Girls weren't much better at any age, he thought a little while later as he drove her home. He'd certainly never figured them out.

"Thanks for a wonderful time," she said as he walked her to her door. "I really enjoyed it."

"So did I," he answered more truthfully than he would have liked. He had to bite his tongue to keep from suggesting they do it again.

"And thanks for the reassurance," she added as she unlocked her door and opened it. "You're right. I know perfectly well that youngsters that age aren't always thinking clearly. They get a wild idea and follow through."

"Still, we have to put the brakes on it. And we will."

She was still smiling as she said good-night and closed the door.

He walked back to his truck, keys jingling in his hand, and thought about it all, from the bullying to the rat to the evening just past. The thoughts were still rumbling around when he got home.

Something wasn't right. Something. He'd grown up here, gone to school here, been away only during his college years, and now had been teaching for a decade.

His nose was telling him something was wrong. Very wrong. The question was what. And who. He didn't want Cassie to be needlessly scared, but he couldn't lay his own concerns to rest.

Somehow, in some way, a scale had tipped, leading to some ugliness against a teacher that was so unusual around here it couldn't be ignored.

What happened to James Carney concerned him, of course, but that fit better into the parameters of the kind of ordinary ugliness people were capable of. It had a frame of reference, one they needed to put a stop to, but well within the range of "normal," however wrong.

Threatening phone calls and dead rats. If it had just been the rat, he would have been almost positive it was someone's bad idea of a prank. But added to that phone call, he couldn't begin to dismiss it.

Nor could he stop wondering if the real problem wasn't students at all now.

# Chapter 4

Cassie's apprehension eased over the next few days. Nothing untoward happened, James was back in class looking all right, if a bit edgy, but when she tried to talk to him as he was leaving, he gave her an angry look and hurried away. Things were still not right in his world, and that troubled her. She wondered if he was still being hassled, but she had no way to know.

On the bright side, her students had come up with some interesting ideas for projects. As she taught them math with some physics mixed in, she enjoyed their pleasure and growing interest.

Success was sweet. She hoped it lasted.

So maybe the worst of the dustup was over, at least for her. Maybe whoever had been mad at her had finished venting. The detentions were scheduled for Thursday afternoon and Les had insisted on supervising them. After Monday, he said, he didn't want her involved with the disciplinary action.

She was, however, involved with Linc in a meeting with the students whom he had approached to become the vanguard in the antibullying campaign.

As she would have expected of the students who were most respected among their peers, they were all good-looking. At that age, appearance meant a lot. But as she listened to them talk with Linc, keeping mostly quiet herself, she was impressed with how good-hearted they were and their quick grasp of the problems.

She knew they'd been handpicked by Linc, and there were probably other student leaders he hadn't chosen, but this group was great.

"There's always bullying," said one of them, a petite blonde named Marcy. "Always. But not like what they did to James Carney. What's wrong with James, anyway? He's just a nerd." And from that statement, Cassie realized the story of what had been done to James had made it all over school. The students were talking about it, so they needed to turn that talk to a positive end.

Linc responded. "There's nothing wrong with James. The question is what is wrong with people who would treat him that way, and whether the student body is going to allow bullying of any kind to continue. The teachers can crack down, but you know where that gets us."

"Yeah," said Bob, a young linebacker from the football team. "It just goes under the radar or happens out of school. That's no good."

"So," said Linc, posing the question, "how do we make bullying uncool?"

"Speak up and speak out," was the first answer from another of the girls. "And we've got to get our friends to do it, too."

"Police it," agreed a boy. "Maybe form a group of students who are willing to step in if they see it."

"Like hall monitors," someone else suggested.

"Diss it," said yet another young man.

At that point, Cassie was moved to speak. "We've got to be very careful not to let our attempts to stop bullying become bullying themselves."

The boy eyed her ruefully. "That makes it harder."

She had to laugh. "You bet."

The important thing was that the conversation had begun, and these students were going to start getting the word out. Specific actions seemed to be beyond reach, other than expressions of disapproval, but that disapproval could spread like ripples.

After the students left, Linc remarked he needed to get ready for practice. "Are you walking home?"

"No, I brought my car today. I need some groceries."

"Okay, then. Have a good evening."

She picked up her book bag and headed out to the faculty parking area, feeling almost amused. No point in feeling hurt by it, but after letting her into his life—even in a small way—on Monday evening, Linc had pulled back like a turtle into its shell.

Oh, he was pleasant, but the distance was back.

How did you figure a man like that? she wondered as she pulled out of the lot. Monday night had been a lot of fun. She'd enjoyed the animals, liked helping with them, and enjoyed his company. Had she done something wrong?

She supposed she would never know. Whatever it was with Linc, she was beginning to think it was his problem, not hers. Which in itself ought to cheer her up. It was a far cry from her usual reaction, that she must be to blame for the way men lost interest.

Heck, she thought with a near giggle, he'd never really been interested in the first place. Maybe she ought to take his aversion as some kind of compliment—aversion was a long way removed from indifference—because clearly she was having an impact on him.

Just not the kind of impact she would have liked.

Unfortunately, Monday night had not just been fun. He'd managed to stir her interest in him beyond being attracted to his good looks, to being attracted by the kind of guy he seemed to be—a man of many talents and interests who appeared to have a good heart. The kind who were usually married with children by the time they crossed her path.

Much as she tried to get her thoughts to behave, to focus on work, teaching, the bullying program and settling into her new place in the world, Linc kept drifting through them. When he did, all other concerns vanished. She'd wander off into some girlish daydream in which he somehow wanted her, wanted to be with her.

Ah, she was getting too old for this. That kind of thinking was better suited to the kids they had just met with, not to a grown woman who'd already experienced her share of dings and knocks from dating. She even had a few permanent dents, so why wish for the unobtainable?

It struck her that wishing for the unobtainable might be a way of keeping herself safe. Oh, boy, she hoped she wasn't that far gone.

She had just climbed out of her car and started walking toward the store when an angry woman approached her. Cassie judged her to be about forty, showing signs of too much sun and wind, with hair almost as dry as straw. A ranch wife? she wondered.

"You!" The woman said the word sharply, taking her hand off the handle of her cart to wag a finger at Cassie.

Startled, Cassie stopped. "Yes?" she said uncertainly.

"It's your fault my boy is on detention today. I know my boy. He never shoved you. You'd better watch your step, lady, because if you want to lie about my kid, you won't be in this county for long."

Cassie's jaw dropped. She didn't know what to say. Les hadn't wanted her to bring James into it, but she hadn't expected him to tell the parents that those boys had shoved her. They hadn't been that forceful, even though the way they had brushed her had felt like a warning of what they could do. She thought Les was just going to say that they had defied her authority.

"Ma'am…" But what exactly could she say? Before she could marshal her words, the woman was storming away, cussing in a low voice.

Well, wasn't that lovely, she thought, her mood souring as she headed into the store. She wasn't going to chase that woman across the parking lot and have a public fight with her, and even if she thought of anything to say that didn't involve what had happened to James, it wouldn't matter. Clearly the woman had made up her mind. She wondered if one of the other teachers would be able to identify her by description.

But did she really want to know?

Damn. Sighing, she pulled a cart from the line, yanking with more force than necessary, and tried to school her face to a pleasant expression as she walked into the store.

She felt a change inside, though. Almost like the way you could feel your ears begin to respond to changes in altitude in an airplane. As she entered it was impossible not to notice that the store was quieter than usual. That people looked at her. That the usually friendly expressions weren't there.

So the parking-lot lady must have been talking.

Her mood sank even more. It would have been nice to just walk out. This would pass, after all, unless those bullies got themselves into trouble again. It was just a detention, no big deal. So she paused to look at a display near the door, one that held no interest for her, and tried to ignore the way her neck prickled with uncomfortable awareness. She could almost feel eyes boring into the back of her head.

Then, as if someone threw a switch, the store returned to normal. Carts started squeaking up and down aisles, a baby cried, women's voices resumed speaking. Employees made noise as they stocked shelves.

Had she imagined that half minute of disapproving silence? Had it even lasted that long? Gripping her cart she set out to get the items she wanted for dinner that night. She had most of what she needed, but when possible she liked fresh vegetables for this dish, and she needed milk regardless.

She received smiles and nods from some of the women as she went, but they seemed tight and forced. She must be imagining it. Surely this many people couldn't be upset about a detention?

Then she remembered the woman's claim that she had lied about being shoved. Well, that would do it, she thought bitterly. If these women believed that, she couldn't blame them.

She was picking through bell peppers, trying to find a few just crisp enough, when a frail voice got her attention.

"Honey."

She turned and found a tiny lady, who could have been any age from sixty to ninety, standing there looking at her from faded blue eyes. "Don't pay it no mind, honey," the old woman said. "Most of us know that Hastings boy and when folks stop being mad they'll think about it. And they'll know he probably *did* push you."

"It wasn't exactly…" Cassie started to explain, but the woman cut her off.

"You stood up for my grandson, James," she went on. "That'll get around, too. Count on it."

Cassie caught her breath. "It might make it harder on him," she protested.

"He's been bullied since he first started school. It's just that way for some kids. Never figured out why. Sometimes it's like watching sharks smell blood in the water. Lately I guess it's getting worse."

Cassie faced her, peppers forgotten. "I want to help him, but I don't know how."

"That's the thing, isn't it? We've been trying to figure out how to help for years. Might as well try to stop a flood with a broom. My daughter and her husband moved away from here for about ten years, so James didn't grow up here. But he got bullied wherever he went, so it's not just this place. You keep that in mind."

Before Cassie could say more, the woman turned away, apparently done with the conversation. How was keeping that in mind supposed to help? She'd been teaching long enough to know that bullying was a sad fact of life for most students. What had been learned about it over the past few decades, however, made it something that couldn't be ignored.

Students were often permanently scarred by even minor incidents, and when the bullying persisted they could de-velop posttraumatic stress disorder. It could lead to depression and even suicide, or violent outbursts. In short, it couldn't be ignored as "just being kids."

She was no fool, however. Bullying could never be entirely stopped or prevented, but that didn't mean that it couldn't be reduced.

There was, however, the basketball championship involved here. Remembering her conversation with Les last Friday, she still felt a burst of frustration that he'd chosen not to exercise the full penalty. His reasoning made sense, but he'd chosen to give the students a slap on the wrist and right now she had a sickening feeling that wasn't helping anything at all, least of all James.

But it was clear from what his grandmother said that he had the support and concern of his entire family. They might consider the bullying inevitable for him, but they weren't ignoring it. That was a step in the right direction, she supposed.

She gathered her groceries and headed for the checkout, where she got a frosty smile from a cashier she had dealt with before.

"Trying to change the town?" the woman asked. "You should live here a while first."

Something inside Cassie snapped. "I'm not trying to change the town. I *like* this town. But don't you teach your kids to respect teachers?"

The woman appeared so taken aback that it might have been funny under other circumstances. She looked down at her scanner and started to run the produce through.

"We teach them to respect," she said finally, in a muffled voice.

"I thought so. Sometimes they just need a little reminder. Don't we all?"

The cashier looked up at that, and her smile was a little more genuine. "I guess so. It's just detention."

"Right. And I didn't lie about anything."

There. Feeling better, she gathered her sacks and headed out to her car. Let *that* get around on the grapevine.

She had heard that small towns could be incredibly gossipy, but the reality was beyond her previous experience. In just under a week everyone seemed to know what had happened, and sides were evidently being taken.

Given that she was the new kid on the block, as it were, she suspected most views didn't favor her much. Well, when had life ever been easy?

Cooking dinner for one had been a nuisance until Cassie had wised up and learned to make larger amounts and save some, either freezing the extra or putting it in the fridge for the next night. It made the effort seem more worthwhile.

Consequently, when she answered a knock at her door and found Linc there, she had enough food to feed him and two more like him. "Come on in," she said, no longer caring if he avoided her or she might be smarter to avoid him. Something about the encounter in the grocery store had fed her courage and self-esteem. "If you have time. I have dinner almost ready."

He hesitated. She almost wanted to sigh with impatience. Couldn't the man just make up his mind? It would be easier on them both. But then she warned herself that she didn't really know what was going on with him.

"You must be hungry," she remarked. "You just came from practice, right?"

He nodded. "I wanted to tell you something."

"Well, tell me inside. My pasta primavera isn't going to be very good if the pasta overcooks."

He followed her into the kitchen while she wondered at how he seemed to blow hot and cold. Just as she waved him to a seat, the timer for the boiling pasta sounded. "Give me a minute," she said as she turned off the stove.

Lifting the colander out of the boiling water, she turned it slowly, allowing it to drain thoroughly. Then she dumped the pasta into a waiting serving bowl.

"That's a lot of food," he remarked.

"I cook multiple meals at a time. Unfortunately, this one doesn't freeze well, so unless you help me out, I'm going to be eating this for the next three or so days."

"It sure smells good," he said.

She took that as agreement and pulled two bowls out of the cupboard, placing them on the table with flatware. "So what was so urgent it couldn't wait until morning?" She put the other ingredients in with the pasta and began tossing the mixture. Keeping her back to him made it easier. At least he wasn't distracting her.

"Talk. There's a lot of talk."

"About the detentions? I heard some of it at the grocery."

"I'm sorry."

She sprinkled Parmesan on the mixture, then carried the meal to the table. "Help yourself," she said, offering him the pasta scoop.

He apparently did like the aroma, because he put a healthy serving into his bowl. "I never go to this much trouble for myself."

"I didn't use to, either." She sat, passing a paper napkin to him, and took a smaller portion for herself. "I was confronted by a woman in the parking lot. It wasn't pleasant. She accused me of lying about her son pushing me."

"Damn," he said. He hadn't even picked up his fork, and when she at last forced herself to look up from her own dinner and meet those amazing blue eyes, she saw genuine concern.

Looking Linc in the eye, she decided, was a dangerous occupation. Every time she did, she felt hormones and hunger surge in a tidal wave that wanted to drive everything out of her head. Her thoughts wandered to those broad shoulders, encased by his Western shirt, and her palms itched to touch him.

No, it was safer to look down at her supper. No wonder eye contact was considered dangerous in so many cultures.

"How bad was it?" he asked.

"Bad enough. Ugly. It wasn't much better in the store. A cashier sort of confronted me. I probably should be ashamed to admit it, but I took her on."

"Good for you."

"So is that what you wanted to tell me?"

"In part," he admitted. "Somehow the whole story has gotten out, and it's not entirely accurate. Gossip never is, but you might say lines are being drawn."

"Against me."

She dared to meet his gaze again and saw tightness around his eyes. "Yes."

"Because no one really knows me yet. I heard that today, too. I'm being seen as an interfering outsider. So what exactly did you hear and from whom?"

"Some of my players. I overheard them talking and inserted myself." He shook his head. "I can't believe all this over a few lousy detentions, but I gotta say that I think Les may have handled this all wrong. People want that championship. I know it probably seems like a minor thing to you…."

"Actually no. And especially not here. I've been in much

more populous areas and larger schools where champion-
ships became really huge. It wasn't always pretty."

He gave her a short nod. "Exactly. Folks here love this
place, they're mostly happy living here, but occasionally
they need something to be proud of. Our football team
seldom wins, but every so often, amazingly enough, our
basketball team takes us to the brink of doing something
that will make a lot of chests puff up."

"That's understandable." She ate another mouthful,
waiting, and wishing her stomach hadn't decided to start
doing flips again. She'd felt pretty good after she'd told
that cashier the truth, but now she was definitely feeling
the first icy fingers of worry and maybe even fear. Did
she really need to be afraid? "So what did Les do wrong?"

"He should have told the parents the whole damn story
and explained that he was going lightly. Instead he focused
on you. So there's talk running around that you lied about
being shoved...."

"I never said I was shoved."

"I know. But apparently Les said you had been. Or made
it sound that way. He should have just left it that you'd been
defied after giving the students a legitimate direction. Or
he should have explained the entire situation. Now nobody has the truth, and speculation is rife. You lied. You
didn't lie. These students wouldn't do such a thing. And
then somebody put it out there that James was being bullied. God knows who. So right now you look like a trou-
blemaker, and folks are wondering why there's a ruckus
about something that all kids do and experience."

She put her fork down, losing all desire to eat. "That's
the perception we have to change."

"Obviously. What's worrying me is that we've barely

begun and people are reaching the wrong conclusions. They're finding it easier to blame you for some transgression than to believe these students could have done something wrong. And now parents are starting to rumble."

Her mouth turned dry. "Already? A detention and they're that angry?"

"They don't know you yet, so they don't trust you."

"But surely kids get detention all the time!"

"Some do. Not these four. It would help if they were the usual suspects."

"God!" She'd never been one for drinking. The wines she kept, although good ones, were something she usually reserved for cooking, but now she rose, dug out two wineglasses, and poured some pinot grigio for each of them. "I hope you like wine."

"With a meal like this, definitely."

She stared at her wineglass, wondering if it was a mistake. Her mother had dealt with life's problems by drinking too much, and it wasn't a habit she wanted to fall into. But right now... Sighing, she sipped then put the glass down beside her bowl.

"I can't eat," she said, somewhere between hopelessness and anger. Some middle ground where no matter which way she looked, her stomach did another flip. "Tell me not to make too much out of this."

"I wish I could. I didn't come over here because I wasn't worried."

"Damn it," she said. "Maybe I should just take myself out of the picture. Ask Les to let me out of my contract and find another job."

"Are you that afraid?"

She bridled instantly. "No!" She glared at him. "I didn't

come here to tear this town apart, but it seems to be what's happening from what you say."

"It'll settle," he said firmly. "It'll calm down. I just wanted you to be aware. You might hear some more ugly things."

"I can take people saying ugly things. What I'm not going to be able to take is another dead rat on my desk!"

He didn't say anything for a minute or more. Something in his gaze said he had more on his mind than the talk going around. Something almost sad.

"If you're going to cut and run," he said finally, "do it now."

Startled out of her self-preoccupation, she gaped at him. "What do you mean by that? I'm just talking because I'm upset. Can you promise me no more rats?"

"I'd like to, but at this point I don't know. I wouldn't have expected the first one. I told you. Some kid playing a prank."

"But now you're not so sure."

He threw up a hand. "I'm not sure of anything right now. I've never seen this place polarize so fast. I can't figure out what the hell is going on. Everyone knows bullying isn't good. Everyone. They just turn a blind eye because it's perceived as kids' stuff. Now we have a crazy uproar over you because kids got detention for defying your authority. I can't explain it. It's like someone put loco weed in the water."

She lifted her glass then set it down and pushed it away. That wasn't going to help anything. Rising from the table, she paced the kitchen, trying to get a handle on this.

He was right. It seemed crazy. But she doubted that many people around here were crazy. So what the hell?

"Somebody," she said after a couple of minutes, "must be lying about something. In an inflammatory way."

"I'm beginning to wonder about that."

"But you didn't hear anything from your players that might explain it?"

"Not a thing. Just that folks are talking."

"People talk. If that's all they do, it'll settle down. The detentions were today. If there are no more, it'll go away."

"I hope so."

She stopped and faced him. "What?"

He shrugged. "If someone wants to get even with you for this, they'll try to provoke another situation."

"I'm not that easy to provoke. Usually."

Then she leaned back against the counter, wrapping her arms around herself as if they could protect her. As upset as she had been by the bullying she had stumbled on, she was even more upset now. "I was just trying to do the right thing, Linc. Not infuriate half the town and threaten a championship."

"I know."

Her eyes felt hot as she looked at him. "I'm the one being bullied now. I just hope I diverted them from James."

Linc was touched by her concern for James, but he couldn't deny that she was the victim now. Someone was deliberately exaggerating this entire affair and he couldn't for the life of him figure out why. He suspected at least one of the bullies' parents was mad about the detention and unwilling to believe their son could have pushed a teacher. Parents had that kind of blind spot as he knew only too well, but this seemed extreme. Then, too, the fact that the initial bullying of James had gotten out, when Les had tried so hard to keep it under wraps for the kid's sake, left him wondering about the dimensions of this storm.

Cassie stood there, looking lost and alone and upset, and there wasn't a damn thing he could do to make her feel better. She'd have to ride this storm out or leave town. She'd already mentioned the possibility herself, a reminder that had left him feeling warned.

Knowing he was being a fool, but doing it anyway, he rose and went to gather her into his arms. The instant he drew her close, he realized he might have just made the biggest mistake of his life.

Those luscious curves he'd been trying to ignore felt even better than he'd imagined. Womanly and welcoming, they seemed to meld right into him. She smelled so good and after the briefest hesitation, she leaned into his embrace and rested her head in the hollow of his shoulder.

"You're not alone in this," he said, hating the way his voice had thickened, giving away the surge of desire that roared through him. He tried to keep his hips away from her, afraid his body was revealing too much as he hardened. Damn, he'd meant to offer comfort, and if she felt his arousal she might be completely put off.

Although that would be for the best, said some nagging voice he didn't want to hear. Being deserted once by a woman who couldn't handle life here had been enough. He couldn't endure that again.

But neither could he refuse Cassie whatever comfort he could offer. It wasn't in him to ignore another's distress. He just wished his whole body hadn't started humming with need. It made the comfort he was offering seem like a sham, and it reminded him of his own terrible weakness.

He wanted this woman, had wanted her since he first laid eyes on her. She had begun to haunt his thoughts and sometimes even his dreams. If he could be sure a simple roll in the hay would settle it...

But he couldn't be sure. It wouldn't be fair to her anyway.

She leaned farther into him, almost resting in the shelter of his arms. Then, slowly, her own arms found their way around his narrow waist.

God, he'd forgotten how good it felt just to be hugged. The warmth of her embrace reached deep inside him, adding to the heat he already felt, but even more dangerously filling some empty hole in him.

Damn, life could be unfair, making him want what he was pretty sure he couldn't have. Making him want another woman he probably couldn't trust. Making him want all kinds of things that weren't his to take or enjoy.

A better man would have stepped back then, feeling he'd made his point that she wouldn't face this alone. But he was not a better man. The desire pounding in him weakened him, and drove caution to the background.

He was certain he'd pay for this, but that couldn't stop him. Need brought him to his emotional knees so fast he couldn't grasp at the straws of sanity.

He needed. He wanted. Before he even knew what he was doing, he tipped her face up and kissed her.

She tasted faintly of the wine she had sipped. Running his tongue along her lips, he felt their full, silken smoothness and then, so unexpectedly, she opened to him and he dove in like a bee seeking nectar. Warm, almost hot, soft like her secret depths. The pounding in his body grew until he could hear the throb in his ears.

It was as if hot ocean waves washed over him, carrying him farther and farther from the security of land. Her breasts, full and inviting, pressed against his chest, and his hands wanted so badly to wander her curves, learning each and every one of them. He could have happily drowned in her.

But at that instant, her body wormed closer and made full contact with his pelvis. The ache that shot through him was overwhelming, but just as they made that intimate contact, she gasped and arched backward. His eyes snapped open and he gazed into hers, seeing surprise, seeing his own heat answered.

It was the surprise that tossed him back on shore to safety. This shouldn't have happened. No way. Nor did he need to review his sensible reasons once again.

He loosened his hold on her, slowly so she wouldn't feel rejected, but as he backed away, he couldn't mistake the brief flicker of hurt in her green eyes.

Well, damn him all to hell for a fool. All he was trying was to keep either of them from being hurt, and he'd gone and hurt her anyway.

He didn't know what to say. He couldn't exactly explain that a momentary madness had overtaken him. Couldn't possibly tell her he didn't trust her to stay in this town and he wasn't traveling that painful path again. Couldn't say, "Gee that was nice, how's the weather?"

If he'd ever had any finesse, he'd just blown it.

But then she rescued him. A smile, a bit uncertain, a clearing of her gaze, a toss of her beautiful hair. "Wow," she said. "But I only just met you."

The line was so obviously intended to lighten the moment of near-disaster that he felt a load lift. "True," he agreed.

She walked back to the table and settled as if she intended to eat. "Don't worry about it," she said calmly. "A kiss is just a kiss and I have no expectations."

That, he thought, as he returned to finish the cooling dinner with her, sounded as if it went beyond a dismissal to a deeper emotional truth for her.

She had no expectations? What did she mean by that? Then he reminded himself it was better if he never found out.

## Chapter 5

Cassie awoke in the morning feeling half-dead. It hadn't helped that she'd lain awake half the night bouncing between remembering an incredible kiss and worrying that people were talking about her and that they suspected she had lied about a student.

The worst of it was she couldn't tell which upset her more. Along about two in the morning, she decided it was the kiss. Bad enough to know the man didn't really want to get close, but now she knew indelibly just how his hard body felt against hers, which only fed the fire of desire he awoke in her with such ease. Darn, it had been like opening Pandora's box.

Come morning, she sat bleary-eyed over her coffee, not at all eager to get to school. She tried to sort through an emotional tangle that seemed to be knotting ever tighter. She wanted Linc, admittedly. He didn't want her. The kiss had astonished her, coming after all the distance he had tried to dig between them like a canyon gorge, but it wasn't the first time someone had been attracted to her and then dropped her like a hot potato.

Story of her life, she thought dismally. Somehow she attracted men, and then she turned them off. She didn't know how or why, but they never stayed long. It seemed they found her initially sexy, and then their interest stopped. Boom.

So it shouldn't surprise her Linc had reacted like every other guy who had made an advance. In some way she couldn't discern, and that none of her friends had ever been able to explain, she put men off after the initial attraction.

She ought to be used to that fact by now.

Then there was this mess at school. Sighing, she stared into her coffee and decided to add some milk to it. Her stomach felt uneasy and the coffee was giving her heartburn. She knew better than to try to go without it, though. Coffee had for years been the thing that stood between her and some very bad headaches. A doctor had even recommended it when she didn't want to take something stronger.

So she swallowed her coffee reluctantly with some dry rye toast and pondered how everything could look so different in such a short space of time. At her age that should come as no shock, but it was still surprising.

A week ago she'd been practically buzzing with happiness about teaching and living here. Now she was dreading the day ahead. She had been confronted by a parent, had seen disapproval from people she didn't even know, and now she wondered what she was going to run into in the classroom today. How many of her students would take a cue from a parent or friend?

Well, there was only one way to find out. Rising, she

rinsed her dishes, grabbed her book bag and a jacket and set out.

Conard County offered her another absolutely gorgeous day, although it had grown considerably chillier than a week ago. Ordinarily the air would have invigorated her, but this morning her feet felt like lead.

Lack of sleep, she told herself, only half believing it. Then a thought occurred to her and she quickened her step. It was time to find out *exactly* what Les had told those parents. If he had told parents she had been shoved, she wanted him to take care of it. If he hadn't, then she would know the problem stemmed from elsewhere. How that would help, she wasn't certain, but she didn't want to also wonder about Les.

She knew Gus, the janitor, would be waiting for her outside her classroom. He was there every morning now, a kind of sentinel, and he always checked out the room before she entered. Unlike some around here, he didn't seem to suffer from an overwhelming belief in the goodness of everyone.

That was a cynical thought, and she yanked herself sharply away from it. One person. A small handful. No more than that. If people had heard a lie about her, then their disapproval wasn't a bad thing. They were rallying around neighbors. That was good, right? Eventually, after this mess was over and enough time had passed, she hoped to be one of the neighbors folks around her would want to protect.

Linc wasn't outside. Evidently he'd completed his turn at bus duty and an English teacher, Carl Malone, had taken over. He greeted her pleasantly. Whatever was going around on the grapevine, it hadn't affected him yet.

For the first time she wondered how many of the teachers might start turning frosty, even though the situation had been explained at the meeting this past Monday.

She was not in the best of moods by the time she reached the principal's office and her mood didn't improve when she saw Linc already inside with Les.

Memories of the kiss came rushing back, and with it an unwanted warm weakness between her legs. Damn, she hated that he could make her want him so much when he clearly didn't reciprocate the feeling. He saw her through the glass, though, and waved her in.

She trudged around the large reception desk and entered Les's office.

"I guess you had the same idea I did," he said. "I was just asking Les exactly what he told those parents."

Les, seated behind his desk, looked both annoyed and defensive. "I didn't tell anyone that those students shoved Cassie," he snapped. "I don't know where that's coming from."

"What exactly did you tell them?" Cassie demanded.

"That you had told them to report to my office for a legitimate reason and they refused. Not one word more than that, except to say we couldn't allow students to defy a teacher's legitimate authority."

"You're sure?" Linc asked.

"I'm not an idiot. Details aren't necessary for the very reason you're in here complaining about."

Cassie looked between the two men. "Then what started it?"

"Probably one of the students involved, or one of their friends," Les said. "A lie, pure and simple, exaggerating the matter."

"I still think," Linc said firmly, "that you should have told everything to the parents, including the bullying."

"I was trying to protect James Carney from retaliation!"

"So now a good teacher's reputation is being impugned. You need to call those parents back and tell them what Cassie saw."

"No," said Cassie, surprising herself. "No. It's over as far as those students are concerned. They had detention and the case is closed. Telling the parents about the bullying will only make them madder, and I'll probably be accused of lying about that. Leave James out of it."

Linc faced her. "Are you sure? This thing has been handled poorly, if you ask me. We need to address all the issues involved with all the students involved."

"Of course," Cassie agreed. "But arguing with people over their current presumption isn't going to help." She shook her head a little. "I admit I wanted to know exactly what Les had told the parents, but obviously he didn't say anything to start this kind of extreme talk. So it had to be a student or parent exaggerating the matter, claiming I lied about what happened. No one can prevent that."

"I prefer to take most bulls directly by the horns," Linc admitted. "But you're right. We can't call back the lies. At this point all we can probably do is avoid inflaming things until we get our presentation ready and get the new policy moving."

"We have a policy?" Les said, bridling.

"We're going to try to get students involved," Linc said. "To get some of the most popular students to start frowning on bullying of any sort."

"Oh." Les stroked his chin. "I wonder if that will work."

"It has in other schools," Cassie said. "Unfortunately, it usually starts earlier than high school. It takes time to grow a culture."

"Well, I don't like the one that seems to have sprung

up here at all. I'm going to take whatever action I deem necessary. You guys have a few weeks. If we have another incident of any kind, I'm cracking down."

Outside in the hallway, Cassie started for her classroom, knowing that Gus was probably still standing there like a palace guard.

"So he's going to crack down," Linc remarked. "I don't know how much that'll help."

"I guess it depends on how many get rebellious."

"At this age, that'll probably be quite a few. Cassie…"

She looked at him then and sensed where he was trying to go. "Forget about it, Linc. Things happen. I need to get to my room."

Hard words to say, but the best way to handle it. She left him quickly, striding away as fast as she could walk. Trouble. There'd be nothing but trouble if she got in any deeper with that man. Regardless of whether his reluctance grew from something in him or something about her, or a combination of both, it didn't matter. It boded badly, and it was time to stay away.

"All clear," Gus said cheerfully when she appeared. He opened the door and waved her in.

"Thanks so much, Gus. I really appreciate your concern."

"No problem. I see more than a lot of people would like. What you're doing is right."

Well, at least she had her own cheerleading section. The thought brought the first smile of the day to her face.

Nor was the day bad. While she had expected there might be some trouble with her students, they all seemed to behave perfectly normally. James Carney still looked isolated and a bit pinched in the far back corner, but that wasn't a change. She just hoped that someday soon he would start to appear more comfortable.

For now all she could do was avoid drawing any attention to him that might bring on more teasing.

Unpleasant though it was for people to be talking about her and thinking she might have lied, it was far better for the attention to be on her. She could handle it. Well, except for butchered rats. The memory nearly made her shudder, but then she reminded herself nothing else had happened. The mood must be cooling down now, at least with whoever had killed the rat and phoned her. The confrontation in the parking lot was still fresh in her mind, but she could deal with that kind of thing.

It was shadowy threats from unknown persons that bothered her most of all, and those had stopped.

By the end of the day she was feeling considerably more cheerful about life…well, except when it came to Linc. The memory of his kiss plagued her, popping up without warning, and unwanted.

Damn, she thought, it was just a kiss. Maybe the nicest kiss of her life, the most arousing—how in the world could she explain that?—but it was still just a kiss. He hadn't taken it one step further. Meaningless. Utterly meaningless.

Except she had felt his response to her, and the memory of *that* kept drizzling through her body like warm honey. He *had* wanted her, if only physically. Supposedly that didn't mean much with men, but it meant a lot to *her*. It was good for her ego, if not her peace of mind.

At the end of the day, Linc appeared in the doorway of her classroom just as she was tucking the last items in her book bag.

"Let's go get a bite," he said.

She looked at him uncertainly. "Why?"

"Why not?" He shrugged one shoulder, reminding her abruptly of the strength in the arms that had held her last night. "We go out to Maude's. Everyone can see you with me. That may lead some folks to question certain assumptions about you."

Another rescue mission. God, she thought as she picked up her bag and tossed it over her shoulder, she wished he'd turn up sometime for another reason. Of course there was that crazy trip out to his ranch on Monday night. What purpose had that served?

Only to make her wish she could spend more time there. She'd really enjoyed it. On the other hand, how could either of them be sure she might like it when the novelty wore off? Maybe that was part of what made him keep a distance.

Deciding there was no point in arguing about it, and silently admitting she *did* want to spend more time with him, she accompanied him out to his truck. There must be neutral things they could talk about, like his ranch and his livestock. Anything but school and bullying. Or desire.

He remained silent through the short drive over to Maude's café. One of the things she found charming in this town was that the City Diner, clearly signed and marked as such, was called Maude's by everyone, after its owner. It had struck her as a signpost indicating how well the people around here knew each other. Learning that had been one of the things that had helped her make her decision to accept this job.

She hadn't really thought about being an outsider, and after Maude had taken their orders in her grumpy fashion, she said so to Linc.

"The one thing I didn't take into my calculations when I fell in love with this county..."

He arched his brows, his blue eyes intent. "You fell in love with this county?"

"Of course I did. I wouldn't have moved here otherwise."

"But how could you know so fast?"

She hesitated, then finally decided to admit the truth. "Somewhere inside I've always looked for a place like this. A small town surrounded by wide-open spaces where most folks are friendly. A place where I could actually get to know most of my neighbors. Silly dream, I suppose, but I dreamed it anyway. Until now I've never lived in a place like this, but I always, always wanted to."

He nodded. "Sorry for the interruption. You were saying?"

"There was one thing I didn't realize, that I'd be an outsider. Maybe for a long time to come. I never had to face that before. So..." She shrugged. "I've learned something. Kids whose families came here to work at the semiconductor plant are still outsiders, from what you said last week. How long have they been here, but they're still the new kids?"

He frowned faintly and leaned back to let Maude serve them coffee. "It's easier with the adults, I think."

"Are you sure?"

At that a faint smile appeared on his face. "Well, when you see what Maude puts in front of you next, you may get the message."

"I didn't order anything."

"Around here, that doesn't matter."

Barely had the words left his mouth than Maude slapped

two pieces of pie in front of them and stomped off without a word. "Pie? Why? What do you mean?"

"Whatever Maude has heard, she's letting you know she doesn't agree with it. You've just been welcomed as a regular here. And that means that sometimes Maude decides what you eat."

"Wow." She looked at the pie and felt warmed. "I'm honored."

"You should be. Some folks have been coming in here for years and never been given free pie."

She looked at him and a little giggle escaped her. "So all is better now?"

"Here at least. Maude's making her opinion known, and my experience is that if she hears any talk about you, some steaks are going to get overdone."

Cassie laughed outright at that. "But why would she have a different opinion from everyone else?"

"I doubt it's everyone else, to begin with. Yes, some folks are talking. It worries me, and I wanted you to be aware of it, but rarely does everyone around here buy something like that as gospel. Who was it who confronted you, anyway?"

"I don't know." And she hadn't wanted to talk about this. "I never met her. Can we discuss something else, please?"

"Sure." He sounded agreeable. "So what's on your mind?"

A lot of things were on her mind, and not a single thing she could mention, really. Ask him about that kiss last night and why he'd pulled away? Not likely. She hunted around inside her head for an innocuous topic while covering her silence with a mouthful of pie.

"Wow," she said. "This pie is fantastic!"

"Maude's famous for them. One of the reasons it means something when she gives you a slice for free."

Cassie looked around and saw Maude walking toward a table. "This pie is fabulous!" she called. "Thank you!"

She supposed that grimace was a kind of smile.

"Not the easiest person to get along with?" she asked Linc quietly.

"Depends. I wouldn't want to be on her bad side, though."

She savored another bite of pie, knowing she'd never enjoy it if they came back to the bullying. "Do you ever think about getting more animals at your ranch?"

He smiled. "Often. I like them. But I have to be realistic about what I can handle. As it is, breeding alone gets ahead of me sometimes."

"Like rabbits, huh?"

"Not quite, but sometimes it feels like it." He rolled his eyes humorously.

"I never thought about raising goats. I can understand all the uses for sheep, but goats?"

"I sell a lot of mine. There's a market for the milk, but also for their hair. Mine are angoras, and their hair is something you'd recognize as mohair."

"Really." She smiled at that. "And their meat?"

"There's a cultural market for that, too. So I really have no trouble making enough off them to pay for them with a little left over. But as a major operation?" He shook his head. "I'd need a lot more than two hands."

"Well, I thought they were neat just to have around. If a few is enough for you, there's nothing wrong with that. I actually liked them better than the sheep."

"They're a lot more amusing, to me anyway. Very smart and full of high jinks. It's a good thing I have the dogs to keep them in line."

The diner was beginning to fill up with people. Cassie looked around, trying to make friendly eye contact, but noticed that a few of the people avoided her gaze. She pushed her pie to one side.

"Don't let them get to you," Linc said quietly. "Stick it out a little longer."

"How's that going to help?"

"I'm here with you. More than any of them, I'm in a position to know whether the gossip is true. Hang in there, Cassie."

"I'm not going anywhere," she said firmly. "But my appetite died."

"Just be sure to take the pie with you."

"Must not offend, huh?"

"You got it."

It was hard not to keep looking at him when he sat right across the table from her. Staring down at her cup didn't feel like the right thing to do, either. The people looking her way could interpret that to mean that she was feeling defensive.

Too much education in psychology, she thought with weary amusement. So here she was, caught between the devil and pair of deep blue eyes, to mangle a metaphor. She could send challenging looks around the room, if anyone was staring, or she could give up and just drink in Linc with her eyes.

She knew what she wanted to do. Seizing on the first straw she could find, she asked him, "Do you have a Celtic heritage?"

"Why do you ask?"

"Because that was the first thing that occurred to me when I saw you. Blue eyes, dark hair." Not to mention an incredibly perfect build from what she could tell. She skipped the part about thinking he resembled a warrior, though. That was definitely over-the-top, a female fantasy not to be shared.

"I guess I do," he said. "My mother always said she was black Irish."

"That would explain it. I'm mostly mutt myself."

He laughed. "You look like anything but a mongrel."

She felt her cheeks flush, but only faintly, thank goodness. "I really don't know much about my family. My dad left when I was three, never to be heard from again, and my mother steadily sank into alcohol."

"Damn, that must have been tough."

She acknowledged it with a nod. "There were good times, too. It wasn't all bad. If I can say nothing else for my mom, it's that I always knew she loved me. No matter what."

"I take it she's gone?"

"A couple of years ago. Cirrhosis."

"I'm sorry."

"No need. It's a horrible addiction and I watched her struggle with it. It was sad to watch, because she tried so hard up until near the end, but it was like watching someone in tennis shoes try to scale the steep side of an icy mountain."

"That's some image," he said quietly.

"That's how it seemed. Like no matter how hard she struggled, she could never quite get her footing. That's why I don't drink much. I'm afraid of it."

"I can see why. I guess I've been lucky, because I never really had to think about it. I can enjoy a beer or two on a weekend, or a glass of wine with dinner, but that's enough for me. I got rousingly drunk once in college and the hangover cured me of any desire to repeat it."

She had to smile. "I hear they're awful."

"I got drunk on wine with some friends. I couldn't stand the smell of the stuff for years. And the morning after..." He shook his head. "Never again."

"I don't like things that make my head feel messed up. I prefer it to be clear."

"Then I guess it would be safe to take you dancing at one of our roadhouses." He winked.

Her heart slammed into high gear. Take her dancing? Surely he was joking. He *had* to be. "Why? Because I wouldn't drink too much?"

"You wouldn't trample my feet," he joked. He appeared to hesitate and then volunteered something she sensed was still a sore spot with him. "My former...girlfriend wasn't much of a drinker until we'd go out to do some line-dancing at a roadhouse just outside of town. Then she claimed the dancing made her thirsty. There was more than one occasion when I practically had to pour her into the truck."

Cassie screwed up her face. "How awful. I'm sorry."

"I made excuses for her. She was just cutting loose, and everyone needs to do that at times. But in retrospect, maybe I should have made fewer excuses."

His face darkened, and she lowered her gaze, deciding to leave him alone. Definitely a sore spot, so why persist? If he wanted to say more, he could.

He surprised her with his next words. "I like to dance. Do you?"

"I'm not very good." Mainly because she hadn't had much opportunity to learn or practice.

"I can help you. Why don't we go tonight, if you can stand the country music? And I promise to get you out of there before things get too rowdy."

She almost gaped at him. Last night he'd kissed her

then backed away as if he felt it was a mistake, and now he wanted to take her dancing? Was he asking her for a date?

No, that wasn't possible. Maybe he just wanted to work off some steam dancing. He said he liked it, and while she imagined he could find women to dance with at the roadhouse, maybe he preferred not to do that. So perhaps he just saw her as a safe dance partner since she was a colleague. "I don't know," she said hesitantly.

"It'll be fun," he assured her. "And it's a part of this county you're not going to see on your own, not if you're wise."

"What does wisdom have to do with it?"

"A lot of people are cutting loose. Like I said, I'll get you out of there before it gets too rowdy."

She got the message, and her curiosity was piqued. She had to admit she wouldn't go to a bar or a roadhouse by herself, and she was willing to bet the flavor of nightspots around here was different than other places she had lived.

Curiosity trumped caution. She had no idea why he'd asked her to go dancing, and feared she might be stepping into something she knew nothing about, but she'd never been afraid to take a little risk. If she had been, she never would have taken this job. "Okay," she said. "But I'm a lousy dancer."

"So are a lot of other people. You won't be alone."

"No practice tonight?"

He shook his head. "We have a game tomorrow. I like the players to have the night off right before when it's possible. I'll pick you up at seven-thirty."

After he dropped her off at home, with directions to wear jeans and comfortable shoes, she puttered around, trying to keep busy while she pondered this strange turn of affairs.

What in the world was going on? Date? Not date? A rescue attempt against the forces of gossip?

She wished she knew.

Linc wished he knew, too. What had possessed him? Last night he'd barely escaped a temptation that had threatened to drown him, and now he was proposing to take the woman dancing?

He'd lost it.

Out in the pastures, tending to his animals and listening to a coyote howl in the distance, he decided he might be getting himself into trouble, which just proved that a grown man could repeat his mistakes, even after painful lessons.

Nor did it make him feel any wiser to remember that she'd been reluctant. Reluctant about dancing, he was sure, but he suspected she was equally reluctant to go with him. He'd had women jump all over such an opportunity before, and he damn well knew when one wasn't jumping.

So maybe it would all be okay. He was doing the neighborly thing, showing her around a bit, at least to places she wouldn't find on her own, like his ranch and a roadhouse. He half expected the atmosphere of the roadhouse would turn her off even more. Smokey, crowded, men talking too loud and telling off-color jokes. She seemed to be the type who'd prefer other amusements. She'd mentioned museums and plays, after all. None of that around here.

So he might as well give her the rest of the county's cold bath: the roadhouse. Which was not to say he had anything against them. After a long, hard week, he didn't see anything wrong with people wanting to unwind in a boisterous atmosphere with a few beers, some twangy music and some dancing. It wasn't as if there was a whole heck of a lot else to do. Church socials if you ran that way, but he didn't, at least not very often. A certain comedian's impression of church ladies hadn't been far from the mark, at least in the church he attended.

Maybe he ought to change that, too.

With goats and dogs nudging him, he almost laughed at himself. Change. That was what he was pining for. At least getting out for a few hours of dancing would be a change from the last couple of years.

It would certainly make some tongues wag in a new way. Everybody around here knew Martha had been his last girlfriend, and everybody seemed to know how it had ended. Martha sure hadn't made a secret of it.

He could imagine the heads shaking as Linc Blair once again took up with an outsider, and by Sunday morning some biddy was bound to suggest he ought to date a local girl. He almost relished the prospect.

Even though the biddy would probably be right.

Aw, what the hell, he thought after he was done tending the animals and had showered and changed. He sat on the back porch for a little while, booted feet up on the railing, and watched twilight take the world.

Almost time to go. He might not know what he was getting himself into here, but there was an unmistakable sense of adventure filling him.

The ranch would never desert him, he thought with amusement. Nor he it. The foundation and cornerstone of his life would always be here, unless he made a stupid financial decision. You really couldn't ask more from life than that.

Everything was chancy by nature, but as long as he had this place, he could take the rest.

Peace filled him, right alongside anticipation. The evening would be fun, even if it never became any more than that. He'd have a chance to watch Cassie in the world she was trying to adopt, and she'd get to see parts of it she might otherwise never really know about.

That might be all it took to snap this fascination he kept feeling for her.

Or not. As usual, only time would tell.

Dropping his feet with a thud, he rose and tugged his keys out of his jeans pocket. Time to go show a lady a good time.


Dusty's Inn didn't look like much of an inn. The large log building was girdled in garish neon announcing any number of brands of beer along with Dancing and Live Music Saturday. The parking lot, consisting of dirt and gravel, held a dozen or so pickups and a couple of cars, leaving room for many more.

"It isn't really busy yet," Linc said as they tooled into a spot next to a pickup that looked older than his. "It'll give you time to ramp up."

She grinned at the expression even though she didn't know exactly what he meant. Excitement and nerves both filled her. "Ramp up?"

"Get used to it. The volume gets a lot worse as the crowd grows. With everyone yammering, Dusty turns up the volume on the music, which makes everyone talk louder. Interesting feedback loop, but I've never been able to convince him there's a point of diminishing return."

Cassie giggled. "Do I need ear protectors?"

"In an hour or two. For now it won't be so bad and I won't keep you past the point where it does."

Keep her? Interesting turn of phrase, she thought as he helped her out of the truck. Did he feel like he was keeping her from something else? Or was that some colloquialism she hadn't yet noticed? Then she reminded herself to quit analyzing and just absorb the experience.

She could hear the music already, even though they hadn't reached the door. The crunch of the gravel beneath her feet made her wish for a sturdy boot rather than her jogging shoes. Judging by the way Linc was dressed, she might well be the only person in the place without a decent pair of boots.

Still it was fun. She was going to a roadhouse in Wyoming on the arm of a cowboy—well, a rancher actually, but tonight she wasn't going to quibble. Not with anything. Some of her old friends would swoon at the mere thought.

Linc always dressed in Western clothes except the couple of times when she'd seen him wearing sweats like the football team. But tonight he'd replaced his battered hat with one in pristine shape, and she thought the toes of his boots looked polished.

Wow. Putting on the fancy duds, she supposed. It tickled her, especially when he had told her to essentially dress down. She had, however, worn her newest jeans, and a satiny green blouse.

She could feel the throb of bass as they drew closer to the building and wondered if it would already be too loud inside.

A plank door opened and a beefy guy in a red T-shirt blazoned with Dusty's welcomed them inside. "It's been a while, Linc." The guy's gaze dragged over Cassie with obvious approval.

"Cassie, this is Glenn. He does his best to maintain order."

Glenn winked at her. "It can be a trial. Nice to see a new face."

They stepped through a second door and the music hit

her like a strong wave. It wasn't deafening by any means, but it was loud. A few couples were already making their way around the huge dance floor, while others sat to one side at tables. A handful dotted stools at the bar that ran around two sides of the room. Through a large doorway to her right, she could see billiard tables.

"This place has everything," she said to Linc.

"Well, it has enough. Let's get a table."

She was glad he didn't immediately suggest taking her onto the dance floor. So few people were out there, she felt she'd be embarrassed. Of course, once it got crowded, she'd probably stick out like a sore thumb.

Then she wondered why she should feel embarrassed at all. Everyone had to learn some time, as she told her students often, and everybody made mistakes.

Linc ordered soft drinks and an appetizer for them.

"You can have a beer," she protested.

"I'm the designated driver."

"And I don't want a beer before I learn how to dance."

He laughed, his eyes crinkling. "A beer might loosen you up."

"How loose do I need to be?"

"For the Cotton Eye Joe? Not a lot. It's an easy dance and a lot of fun. More fun with more people."

"I'm nervous," she admitted.

He reached out and touched her hand lightly. Sparks immediately zinged through her. "It's not hard, I swear. Just watch them dance for a little while and you'll start to feel the rhythm of it. Then I'll show you the steps."

The colas came in huge red plastic glasses, the appetizer in a paper-covered plastic basket. No frills here. She rather liked that. Frills would have seemed so out of place.

"I should have told you to wear smooth-soled shoes," he remarked. "It would be easier."

"Well, I don't have to dance at all."

His blue eyes laughed at her. "You're not getting out of it."

The place slowly filled up with people of all ages. From her limited experience of nightclubs, that surprised her. The few she had visited had seemed to be age-segregated, catering to younger people. This one had the whole range of ages from twenties to sixties or maybe older. She liked that.

As the floor sprouted more dancers, she found her courage. Not that she could have escaped. Linc reached for her hand and pulled her that way.

"It's easy," he said. "Really easy." Keeping her at the edge of the floor, he said, "The first step is stomp-kick-triple step."

She gaped at him, then watched as he did it several times. She could feel eyes on her, but when she glanced around people seemed to be busy with their own companions.

"Now you."

She bit her lower lip and tried to imitate him. The music seemed to help, giving her the rhythm. She made a couple of mistakes, but in a relatively short time thought she had it down reasonably well.

Maybe so, because then he taught her the next part, the shuffle. "Wow," she said finally, "that feels almost natural with the music."

"The whole dance does," he assured her. He slipped an arm around her waist. "Now let's try it. This dance is done side-by-side."

She'd already gathered that part. Feeling a little more

confident, she let him guide her around the edge of the dance floor. With only a few missteps, she made it around the entire circumference. The song changed and they were off again, and pretty soon she stopped thinking about her feet and started thinking about the man whose arm so casually cradled her waist. Stealing a look at other couples, she realized that wasn't a one-way street, so she slipped her arm around his waist.

Wow! It felt so good that she almost closed her eyes with pleasure. Holding him, being held, moving with the music, it all seemed to meld into one wonderful experience.

She was startled back to awareness as she felt an arm link with her free arm. She looked and saw another couple. The man smiled at her and danced alongside her.

Before she knew it, she was part of a line that was pivoting around the dance floor. Then everything shifted, and the whole line was moving straight across the floor, first forward and then backward.

Beneath the loud music, she heard herself laugh. Her head came up, she tossed her hair and grinned at Linc. He grinned back.

She had no idea how long she danced. The songs changed but she didn't count the changes. She was having too much fun. At last, just as she started to feel parched, Linc eased them out of the line and guided her back to the table.

He held out her chair for her, saying, "You're a natural."

"It's fun!"

Fresh soft drinks awaited them, and she drained half of hers in several chugs. He pulled his chair around so that he sat right beside her, rather than across from her.

"So where's this rowdiness that had you concerned?" she asked.

"Later. A different crowd will start showing up, and the beer will flow faster. We'll leave around then."

Just then, without warning or invitation, a heavyset, very large man pulled a chair out and sat at their table. Cassie looked at him in astonishment, wondering if this was another local custom she didn't yet know. She had the feeling she recognized him, but couldn't place him.

"Howdy, Dave," Linc said. "What's up?"

Cassie started to relax as she realized Linc knew him. The relaxation didn't last long.

"So this is the teacher who got the Hastings boy in trouble."

She sensed Linc stiffening, and her own nervousness resurfaced, her stomach feeling almost as edgy as it had right before she'd stepped onto the dance floor the first time.

"I think you got that wrong, Dave," Linc said. To Cassie it sounded as if his voice were edged in steel.

"So she's not the teacher? Everyone says she is."

"What you got wrong is who got who into trouble. The Hastings boy did that to himself."

Dave scowled. "We got a championship to win, Coach. You know that."

It was the first time Cassie had heard anyone call Linc "Coach" except for his team, and she wondered if that word had been chosen for a reason. Of course, in other schools the coaches had been called Coach by everyone. Not here, though, which was odd when she thought about it. Maybe Linc didn't want to be addressed that way?

But her primary concern was Dave. His face was red, and she wondered if he'd had too much to drink. And how far this was going to go.

"I know all about the championship," Linc said. "But the players also know they shouldn't break school rules if they want to play the game. That hasn't changed since your day, Dave."

Dave's expression darkened. "Back in my day, we didn't have no zero tolerance. Kids do things. Kid things."

"That's true. But it's up to us to teach them better."

"Not by blowing the championship. Back in my day, nobody would have risked it."

"Then they were wrong."

Dave shoved back his chair and wagged his finger at Cassie. "You watch it, woman. This whole damn county is going to hold you responsible if we lose because Hastings can't play. And some folks ain't none too sure he bullied that Carney kid or pushed you. Besides, all kids get bullied. I sure as hell did."

He turned and stalked away before another word could be spoken.

Cassie reached for her drink, needing to do something with her hands, only to realize that she was shaking. At once Linc covered her hand with his, and squeezed reassuringly.

"Take a few breaths," he said, the music almost drowning him out. "We'll leave in a few minutes. After we make it clear he's not driving us out."

"I'm not leaving," Cassie argued, hating the tremor she heard in her voice. "I don't like people wagging their fingers at me."

One corner of Linc's mouth lifted. "I'm sure you don't. But Dave is the beginning of the next group of patrons. We wouldn't be staying much longer anyway."

This was the second time in two days that she had been confronted. This thing, she thought, was apt to be like cockroaches. If you saw one, there were probably a quarter million others in the walls. Tip of the iceberg.

The thought almost nauseated her, especially since she doubted that these people would be so angry if she'd lived here all her life. Maybe there was no way to become a real member of this community. Maybe she'd always be an outsider.

She quickly corralled her thoughts, realizing she had edged toward an extreme. Yes, she'd been confronted twice by people who believed she had lied about what had happened. But Maude had given her a piece of pie.

She looked at Linc. "Let's dance again before we leave."

He half smiled. "Sending a message, huh?"

"You bet." Her spine stiffened as she decided that regardless of what came out of this, regardless of whether she began to find it impossible to teach here, she wasn't going to let anyone think she had been cowed. No way.

The dance floor was getting much more crowded, and she noticed the makeup of the clientele had begun to change. More younger people, fewer older ones. The night was just beginning for some.

She also noticed something else: she got pushed. Not hard, not obviously, but unmistakably. Linc, who was on her other side, didn't notice the number of people who suddenly seemed to have developed two left feet, at least when they came near to her. Brushes like the boys had given her last week. Not enough to make her stumble, but they felt like a warning.

She turned her head toward Linc. "Linc?" She had to practically shout to be heard over the growing volume in the room.

He heard, though, and bent his head close to hers. "I'm being pushed. Repeatedly."

His face settled into a frown. "Hold on just a bit longer."

She managed a nod, then realized what he had expected.

Almost as if it were a good-night to the early crowd, the music shifted into something slow and sad. The line dancing stopped and couples turned face-to-face, arms around each other.

Linc pulled her close, an arm around her waist, the other holding her hand up in a traditional dance pose. Slowly he danced her around the floor.

It would have been wonderful if she hadn't been so disturbed. She felt a flare of anger toward the people who had tried to ruin this evening for her, and attempted to think about nothing except that Linc was holding her close, his head bent toward hers.

When she looked into his eyes, she saw blue fire. Regardless of the ugliness, he was thinking about one thing and one thing only. She couldn't miss the message.

Her heart lifted, her lips curved up a bit and she gave herself to the moment, wishing it could go on forever. She reminded herself that he was probably just sending a message of his own, but for the next four minutes that didn't seem to matter.

This time as they left the dance floor to collect their jackets, he didn't hold her arm. He held her hand.

*So take that,* she thought with weak amusement as she saw a few young women look enviously at her. It wouldn't solve the problem, though, nor did she have the least idea what would.

She just knew that while she wanted to get out of here, she also didn't want to go home.

# Chapter 6

Outside in the parking lot, she stopped dead in her tracks, ignoring the steady flow of people around her.

"Is that snow?" she asked, looking toward one of the towering light posts where she was sure she saw a few flakes fluttering down.

"It is," he confirmed. "Just a light flurry, hardly anything at all. It won't stick."

"This is so cool!" she said, forgetting her upset. "I wish we'd get a lot."

A chuckle escaped him as he unlocked his truck and helped her in. "What's the rush? We'll have plenty of winter."

"I want to go cross-country skiing," she said. "I already have the equipment so now all I need is some snow."

"It might be a while yet but the weather around here has been growing much less arid. The last few years we've had more snow than usual, so you might luck out and not need to go up into the mountains to ski."

"Where else would I ski?"

"My ranch is a great place. If there's enough snow."

"No prepared trails?"

"Not around here." He closed the door and walked around to slide in behind the wheel. "Have you ever skied without a prepared trail?" He turned over the ignition and started easing out of the parking lot, avoiding cars and pedestrians.

"Of course, but it's been years."

"I've never had the time to give it any thought. Maybe after the football season is over. You can practice at my place if we have enough snow."

What was going on here? she wondered. After keeping such a distance, he seemed to be closing it awfully fast. Was he just taking pity on her? The question soured her mood, and caused her to reflect on what had happened tonight.

"Those people were pushing me," she said. "Like the boys did last week. Maybe a bit harder."

"But not hard enough that they couldn't claim it was a mistake."

"Exactly."

He wheeled onto the highway and headed back toward town. "I don't like this."

"I don't either, but I can't imagine a thing to do about it. Frankly, Linc, I'm more worried about James Carney. The story of him being bullied shouldn't have gotten out. The fact that it did means someone linked it directly to my complaint. I can't imagine the hell that boy might be going through."

"I haven't seen anything at school."

"Neither have I. He won't talk to me on the phone, either. He told me to just stay out of it. So I have, but…" She bit her lip and looked out the window.

"What can you do, Cassie? We're doing what we can to try to change student attitudes. We'll have an assembly next week."

"Next week? Les didn't mention that."

"Maybe he thought I'd tell you. Regardless, I don't see what we can do. We can't provide protection for James around the clock. We can't follow him to make sure no one bothers him. All we can try to do is make sure these students get it. All of them."

"Do you have any idea how alone he must feel? God, it breaks my heart. His grandmother said he's been bullied everywhere they lived. How much of that can a youngster take?"

"I don't know."

"The statistics aren't good. And can you imagine, everywhere you've lived your entire life being bullied? You'd have to be convinced that something is wrong with you."

"The way you are?"

She gasped, stunned. "What do you mean?"

"Just what I said. Sometimes I get the feeling you think something's wrong with you. Were you bullied a lot?"

She didn't answer immediately, as painful memories flooded back. Had she been bullied a lot? There were all kinds of bullying, some of it as mild as just being excluded. Between being smart and being plump, she'd certainly been made to feel that she wasn't like the other kids. But how much of that was simply normal teenage angst about fitting in? "Some," she said finally. "I don't know if it was a lot. It's not like there's some measuring stick."

"I know."

"Were you bullied?"

"A few times in seventh and eighth grade. It's a rough age for boys. But overall, I'd say not. The fact that you don't know…well, it makes me wonder. How many scars do you carry, Cassie? Do you even know?"

Probably not, she thought miserably. How could she know? She'd had a small circle of friends even at that difficult stage of life. That made her luckier than many. On the other hand, she'd been excluded from a lot, too. Boys hadn't asked her out. Cliquish girls had ignored her. And then there were those who said things about her weight.

"One time," she said slowly, "I was riding the bus back from a basketball game. When it came to a hill, it slowed down and groaned. One of the players shouted out, 'We need to dump some weight from this bus. Make Cassie walk.'"

"Hell. Did that happen often?"

"Things like it, once in a while."

"But often enough. I'm sorry."

She almost said, "But it happens to everyone." That much was nearly true, but that didn't make it right. "There were harder things."

"Such as?"

"My best girlfriend. A lot of the guys wanted to date her, but her parents wouldn't let her date. So they'd ask her on group outings. Her parents wouldn't let her go unless I was there to chaperone. So that's how I got to go."

"You were chaperoning your friend? Good God. That must have made you feel awful!"

"Oddly, I hoped they'd get to like me better if I was enough fun. Being fun evidently wasn't the answer, and I didn't feel too good about it when I realized it."

"You were a lot of fun tonight," he said after a few seconds. "I had a great time. I don't know how you looked in high school, obviously, but I can tell you that right now you're a glorious-looking woman, I was proud to be with you, and you forget those guys who didn't have eyes to see."

Her throat tightened and her eyes grew hot as if tears wanted to flow. She honestly couldn't remember any man saying such a sweet thing to her. "You didn't have to say that."

"No, I didn't. That's the point. I didn't have to say a damn thing."

Now he sounded like he was steaming. She almost said, "You'll change your mind like every other guy," but she held the words in. That was a place she didn't want to go for a bunch of reasons. One night of dancing didn't mean they had a relationship, and she didn't want him to misunderstand what she thought. She settled for "Thank you."

As he pulled in behind her car in her driveway, a few random snowflakes sparkled in the headlights. They were so beautiful. Then she saw her car.

Linc was already quietly furious, though he'd done his best to conceal it. Dave Banks coming up to them like that, Cassie getting pushed on the dance floor, followed by some very personal revelations from her that at once touched his heart and twisted his gut... Well, he was angry. Very angry. When he saw her car he got so mad he almost saw red.

"Don't get out," he said sharply. Pawing around in his jacket, he found his cell phone and called the sheriff's office. Four flats on a car with the back window painted LIAR was not something he was going to ignore. No way. As far as he was concerned, the cops around here needed to get off their butts *now*.

Cassie murmured something. He didn't want to look at her, didn't want to see anguish or fear on her face, not that he would have blamed her for either. He reached out blindly, found her hand and held it tightly.

"Linc, I'm getting scared. Tonight…" Her voice cracked and she didn't finish.

He couldn't blame her. The implied violence in being pushed, however lightly, and now the vandalism to her car would have made any sensible person afraid. "I told you that you wouldn't face this alone. I meant it."

She didn't ask what he meant, and right then he didn't explain. Instead she asked a question that raised every emotional red flag he'd had since Martha.

"What the hell is wrong with this place? I can see people getting angry. I can see people lying, especially when they're upset about their kids. I can see students lying to cover their misdeeds. But to keep brushing me on the dance floor? Those were adults, Linc. And now this."

She had a valid point. "How many people pushed you?"

"Four, maybe five. No more than that. It was carefully done. Some others I was almost sure were accidents."

"Did you see who they were?"

"I saw faces, but I don't know them."

"Younger?"

"Yes."

He turned that around in his mind. "Some people never seem to leave high school even after they graduate. Maybe they were friends of those students."

"I guess."

"I'm just saying that I don't think most people around here would condone that. The vast majority, maybe ninety-nine percent, wouldn't condone that. I'm sorry as hell you met the others."

"Yeah, all in one place." She sighed and turned her hand over so that she was holding his. "Okay, it's probably a very small set. Very small. Most of the people I've met here have been pleasant. And given how many people were dancing when that started, it really was just a few. There must have been a hundred people in that place."

"At least. It's a busy roadhouse on weekends."

"But clearly people around here are mad at me and worried about the championship. Look at that Dave guy."

"So what do you want to do?"

"I don't know. I honestly don't know. But if this keeps up, maybe I should back out of my contract and let the people here deal with it however they want."

He felt an astonishingly strong pang. There it was. "Do you want to leave?" he asked levelly.

"Truthfully, no. But I'm getting scared and I'm wondering what kind of place this really is."

He had no answer for that, especially since she'd only been here a couple of months. How could he defend his county, his neighbors, to her when she had so little experience? It was a relief to see the sheriff's car pull up at the curb.

The random snowflakes continued to fall, almost like a harbinger of things to come.

It would have been so easy, Cassie thought, to decide to pack up and tell Les on Monday morning that she no longer felt safe here. She was sure he would let her out of her contract for that reason.

But even as the desire to get away scrambled around in her head, she had other memories rising up, memories of how pleasant most people here had been to her. How welcoming some of them had been. The pie from Maude today was just one of the incidents that had warmed her since her first day here.

The neighbors who had helped her unload her moving truck, and had been so willing to carry heavy items to exactly where she wanted them. The fellow from two doors down who had mowed her little patch of grass a few times until she found a neighbor boy she could hire. The ladies who had come over with casseroles and other delicacies so she wouldn't have to cook while moving in.

She closed her eyes, focusing on those people and on her fellow teachers who had been nice enough. No, whatever was happening, Linc was right, it involved a small few. While many might be wondering what was actually going on, the truth was, it was only a few who were taking it to the extreme.

But it sure didn't make her feel safe.

The deputy who arrived was a good-looking man in his fifties. Linc introduced him as Virgil Beauregard, but called him Beau. He walked around the car with a flashlight, shaking his head, and squatted down to examine the tires.

"I'm gonna start sounding like our last sheriff," he remarked as he straightened. "This county is going to hell in a handbasket. This about that detention thing?"

"Probably," Linc answered. He sketched the other incidents for Beau, whose frown deepened.

"This seems awfully extreme over a detention," Beau remarked. "It won't keep the kid from playing basketball."

"Nope. Not unless he gets another one."

"Somebody's going to get detention in the county jail if they don't look out." He pulled out a notebook and scribbled. "Whoever they were, they discovered it's harder to puncture a tire than you'd think. Unless there's damage I can't see, they let the air out of the other three after puncturing one. I'm gonna get some other guys out here and we'll talk to neighbors. Maybe someone saw something. It was kind of early in the evening to pull a stunt like this. You all go on inside."

It might be early, but it was also dark, Cassie thought as she led the way inside. Her house also sat in a puddle of shadow between streetlights that weren't terribly bright to begin with.

"Coffee?" she asked, even as she automatically started to make a pot. Somehow she didn't feel as if she were going to sleep tonight, caffeine or no caffeine.

"Thanks." Behind her, she heard the chair scrape as he sat at the table. "You're being awfully quiet about all this."

"What should I do? Erupt? That won't change a thing."

"No, but I wouldn't blame you for being furious."

She started the coffeemaker and joined him, sitting across from him at the table. "Right now I'm frightened. Maybe I'll get angry later. Or maybe I won't. There's nothing that's been done that can't be fixed."

"Except the part about you being frightened."

All too true, she thought, resting her forehead in her hand and drawing aimless circles with her fingertip on the tabletop. "I just wish I knew how far this is going to go, and for how long." Unanswerable questions. "Do you think someone might get violent?"

"A week ago I'd have said no way. I don't even get *this*. A lousy detention? It's not like Ben Hastings can't play because of one detention. If he gets another, or gets suspended, that would be different, but that hasn't happened. All he has to do is behave."

She lifted her head, having noted that he hadn't really answered her question about violence. Her nerves tried to stretch tight, and she drew a deep breath. Violence over a detention? All it would take was one unhinged person. *Stop,* she commanded herself. Get back to reality.

After a minute or two, she spoke again, trying to remain reasonable. "Maybe someone is afraid I'll push the bullying issue. That *should* have got him suspended. He's now on a knife edge, and apparently that's got some people worried." She paused. "One of the teachers must have talked out of school, after our meeting on Monday."

"Why do you say that?"

"How else would everyone seem to know about James Carney? And certainly, having me as part of an antibullying program.... Oh, that was a mistake. I'm the new broom and it probably looks like I'm sweeping through demanding changes, and likely to make a serious issue of future bullying."

"Will you?"

She looked up and saw him smiling faintly. "Yes. I was demanding suspension when I walked into Les's office last week."

"Good. Maybe it takes a new broom to make us realize we need to change some things. When things become too familiar, it's easy to overlook them. Plus, there seems to be a lot of 'kids will be kids' mentality running around. That needs to change about this issue."

She nodded. She had heard the coffee finish brewing, so she went to fill a couple of mugs. "I'm sorry I can't offer much to eat. I don't keep many snacks around and tomorrow is shopping day. Or was. I guess it's going to be car day instead."

"I know the couple who run the auto repair shop. I'll give them a call in the morning and have it all taken care of."

She slid into her seat and made a face. "What if they're on the pro-Hastings side?"

"Whatever side Morris is on, if he's even on one, he'll do a good job for you. Besides, I'll bet most people around here haven't even picked a side. The championship may be important, but most people probably don't consider it important enough to try to mistreat you. I can understand some folks wanting to argue with you, but beyond that..." He shook his head. "It's got to be one person who vandalized your car. The bumps on the dance floor were probably some of Hastings's friends. And I'm trying to minimize this." He gave her a rueful expression. "I guess I shouldn't do that. This is new territory for me."

The doorbell rang. Linc offered to get it, and a minute later he was bringing Beau into the kitchen.

"Coffee?" Cassie asked automatically.

"No thanks. I've had my limit tonight. Okay, neighbors didn't see anything. Some weren't home, others were busy watching TV. As far as they knew, the street was quiet. We're looking around for evidence, but you might as well turn in for the night. Although the floodlights are going to be bright."

"Can I scrape her rear window off?" Linc asked. "I don't want that word there come morning."

Beau hesitated. "I'll do it when we've collected all the information we can." He turned to Cassie. "I'll let you know if we find anything."

"He won't," Cassie said after Beau left. "It's just some vandalism. It hardly requires the sort of investigation a major theft or murder would get."

"You might be surprised. Beau probably feels like you have the entire county on trial in your mind."

"Well, I don't. Not yet. But I may get there if this keeps up."

"Cassie?"

She looked his way. "Yes?"

"You've got a choice. I can camp on your couch tonight or you can come out to my place and use one of the spare bedrooms for the weekend. Either way, I'm not leaving you alone tonight."

She was startled and grateful all at once. "Are you that worried someone might try to hurt me?"

"Hell, I don't know anymore. I never would have thought this much would have happened. But what I do know is you're frightened, with good reason, and that's enough to make me feel you shouldn't have to be alone tonight."

It was all she could do not to gape at him. The turn-around he'd made this week was astonishing. The guy who had tried so hard not to connect with her was now suddenly there, connecting in a myriad of ways. Taking her to his ranch, taking her out to Maude's, dancing and now this?

Part of her screeched to back away before he did. Because he probably would. He must have had some reason for treating her as if she were contagious for the last couple of months. But now he was in her corner, totally and completely.

A white-knight complex? That promised nothing good, because as soon as he felt she no longer needed protection, he might well pull away again.

But she had to admit, the idea of being alone tonight bothered her. She'd lived by herself most of the time since she left college, and never before had it disturbed her, but looking at the night ahead, she really didn't want to be on her own after the deputies finished.

"Pack a bag," he said, making the decision for her. "I've got plenty of room. Plan on spending the weekend. I'll have Morris take care of your car in the morning."

She wanted to object just because she preferred to make her own decisions, but she realized that would be cutting her nose off to spite her face. She *wanted* to spend a weekend at his ranch. She liked it out there. She'd get more of a window on him and how he lived.

And she sure didn't want to stay here. Her home didn't feel as friendly or safe tonight. Nor did sleeping on the couch strike her as very comfortable for him, not as tall as he was.

Finally she nodded and went to pack. Escape sounded so good right now, even if only for a weekend.

The drive to the ranch seemed mysterious along isolated and dark country roads. With the sky clouded over, all she could see was the area illuminated by the headlights and a stray snowflake or two. Even the mountains to the west had vanished, the same inky color as everything else.

"It gets so dark out here at night," she remarked. "I'm used to places where there's at least some light. I didn't know a night could look like this."

"You'll have to come outside with me if the clouds clear out. You probably never saw just how many stars are up there. The first time I really noticed them was when I'd been away at college. Sometimes I think we don't look up often enough."

"Meaning?"

"Maybe we'd realize just how small and unimportant most things are." He paused. "Once we get to the ranch, if you feel like it you ought to sit outside for a while. Let your eyes adapt. With this cloud cover, I can promise you'll see a glow from neighboring ranches. It'll be faint, but you can see it. On a clear night, you can't."

"Maybe I'll try that." Because sleep was the last thing on her mind.

No, with each passing mile her other concerns and fears faded in an increasingly intense awareness of the man beside her. When they had been dancing, there'd been enough going on and enough people around to keep it in check, even during the slow dance when she had wanted to melt against him.

But there was nothing now to keep her mind in check. Not one thing. She was away from town, away from the person or persons who were so angry with her. Safe. And safety awoke a new kind of danger.

Linc felt like throwing up his hands in surrender. He'd failed in every single resolution to keep his distance from this woman. A handful—well probably just a handful, if not just one—of bullies had pushed him right toward her like a plow pushing snow. Nor did he see anyone else stepping up for her. He was still annoyed that Les had put the onus on her for this entire situation. With the best of intentions, he was sure. Who would have expected this kind of reaction?

It remained, his own resolve had failed. He'd known from the moment he first saw her that he wanted her. He thought he knew better, and had made up his mind to stay clear.

Now here he was, taking her to his place for the weekend, a woman who had just tonight mentioned canceling her contract. Leaving. Just like Martha. But even worse,

Cassie certainly had ample reason to wonder if she should remain here.

God, he couldn't fathom this. Not at all. A week ago he would have said this was impossible. People might talk among themselves—well, of course they would. They might even argue about it. Hastings's parents would certainly feel confrontational. But *this?*

He understood the importance of the championship. The school wasn't that big, and didn't have that many students to draw on for its teams. A star came along maybe once every ten or twenty years. In fact, he seemed to remember the last time the school had been in line for a basketball championship had been about twenty years ago. Since then they'd had a track-and-field star, and one football team that had made it to the state playoffs. So yeah, this was a big deal.

Everyone knew scouts had been looking at Hastings. This could be his ticket to college and a very bright future. People were rooting for that kid at least as much as they were rooting for the team. Something bright and wonderful was hovering in the wings, providing a change to the ordinary routine, a few months of pride and something different to talk about.

He could also understand how those who were personally close to Hastings, like his mother and friends, might want to yell at Cassie or even bump her on the dance floor.

But the rat was on a whole different level, as was the vandalism of her car. He'd tried to dismiss that rat to Cassie, even accepting her initial arguments about it, but somewhere deep inside he hadn't been able to shake the feeling they were dealing with a disturbed mind.

Now he was sure of it. People getting into arguments

over the detention, even dismissing the wrongness of bullying the Carney kid, that didn't rise to this level.

Frankly, he admitted to himself, the idea that someone, just one person, was disturbed enough to pull this stuff had him far more worried than if there'd been a mob in the streets. You could deal with a mob. They were out there where you could see them. But one sicko slinking around in the shadows? That's what worried him.

He glanced over at Cassie just before he turned onto his road. She was folded up on herself, staring blindly out the window into the night. It was a good thing the road was bumpy and he had to keep both hands on the wheel. Otherwise he might have wrapped her up in his arms, and then all hell would break loose because he wanted her with an ache as deep and wide as the open spaces out here.

He snapped his eyes back to the road. Danger. The night suddenly seemed to be filled with it, and it wasn't some crazy person he was worrying about. It was himself.

He could do her more harm than some vandal. What she had revealed earlier had told him a lot. He wasn't the only one in this truck with old wounds, not the only one seriously at risk of taking a misstep.

God knew, he didn't want to wound her any more. And he didn't want to go through a replay of the most god-awful months of his life.

She might run. The urge was strong enough that she'd mentioned it, then backed away. All he could do was ensure that neither of them got hurt in any way.

Cassie accepted Linc's hand as she climbed out of his truck beside his ranch house. It was colder, as if the land out here had exhaled the day's remaining warmth faster than the streets in town.

"How'd it get so cold?" she asked, trying to keep this casual. Much as she wanted to fall into his arms, she had decided during the ride that the best thing would be to stay away. He had run cold, then hot, indicating that he had some kind of problem with her. She didn't need to know what it was to realize she needed to keep her distance.

She focused her attention away from him, and tried to quash memories of being held in his strong arms. Tried not to draw a mental picture of those narrow hips and wide shoulders. Tried not to remember the remarkable compliment he had paid her, or the way his blue eyes seemed to heat up when they gazed at her.

The night was suddenly upon them, and although it was cold her internal heat was rising. She couldn't seem to draw enough of the icy air into her lungs. *Don't look at him.* Don't encourage whatever it was that seemed to be filling the short distance between them, that seemed to tug her toward him the way gravity held her to the ground.

"Let's go inside," he said. "I'll make you a hot drink. Then if you want, we can sit out back for a while."

"I'd like that." That sounded safe enough. Sitting outside all bundled up would surely freeze the hot waves of desire that had started to pulse within her. Who could think about sex in the cold, while wearing almost enough clothing for an Eskimo?

Evidently she could, she thought with amusement as she followed him inside.

He left her bag inside the door. "I'll let you pick a room later," he said. Then he led the way to the kitchen, where he made a couple of mugs of instant cocoa.

Outside the temperature seemed to have fallen a bit more. Maybe, Cassie thought, it was just a contrast to being indoors.

He had a wide porch and a number of padded patio chairs that were comfortable. As soon as she settled into one with her mug, he disappeared into the house. He returned a few minutes later with a blanket he tucked around her legs.

"Let me know if you start to feel too cold. I know you just came from a warmer climate."

"Considerably warmer," she admitted. "Occasionally we got down into the low thirties or even twenties, but usually not often enough to get used to it."

"I'd miss the seasons," he said as he settled into his own chair. He put one booted foot up on the railing and looked out into the dark, mug in one large hand.

"I know I did. I wanted to get back to them."

"You hated it?"

"Not really. Not at all. It's just that when I was young, before my mom decided to follow this guy to Florida, I always loved the change of season. Especially autumn. Don't ask me why, but I missed autumn most of all. Down there you usually sense it only by the change in the quality of light. That happens long before it cools down and the leaves change."

"How'd your mom's guy work out?"

"Not too well," she admitted. "It came apart after about six months."

"How did you feel about that?"

"Relieved. He wasn't nasty to me or anything. It wasn't like the horror stories you hear. I just didn't especially like him. He never really tried to like me. I guess I felt tolerated."

He was silent for a while. She realized that he was right, she could see the faint, distant glow from other ranches.

She wondered if it would disappear later, or if they had security lighting.

She heard some soft sounds from the direction of the meadows, but they didn't strike her as disturbed. "Do the animals stay awake all night?"

"No, but they don't sleep like we do. They move around occasionally, and make a little noise."

"It's beautiful out here."

"I think so," he agreed. "Cassie?"

"What?"

"Did you always feel like an outsider, even at home?"

She looked down at the mug she could barely see and felt her chest tighten. "I guess so," she said after a moment. "Doesn't nearly everyone?"

"I don't think so."

"Why did you ask?"

"Thinking about a little girl moving to Florida so that her mother could follow a man she hardly knew. You've changed jobs a lot, too, haven't you?"

"Three different school districts in eight years isn't a lot."

"Maybe not. What are you looking for?"

"I told you. A place like this. Well, a place like what I thought this was."

"You're already thinking about leaving."

She tried to see him, but it was too dark to do more than make out his silhouette. "It crossed my mind. But I'm not going to."

"Why not?"

"Because I really want to put down roots, Linc. *Really*. It's like there's always been this place in my heart where I wanted to live, and life conspired to keep me away from it. I was always in busy metropolitan areas, larger towns.

Places where you could blend in with the walls. I wanted something warmer."

"You can make a community anywhere," he said. "It doesn't have to be geographic."

"I know that. But I want a geographic community. I want to know who lives two blocks over, I want to recognize the people on the streets. I want to be able to greet most of them by name. Most places I've been, you can live in an apartment for a couple of years and barely recognize the people next door. You can rent a house in the suburbs and you'd think the neighborhood was empty. The front-porch culture seems to be gone."

"Not from here," he admitted. "Although those of us out on ranches and farms have to make some effort. It helps, growing up here."

"Are you saying I can't become part of this community?"

"Not at all. It'll happen. You might be referred to as the new teacher for a while, though."

She gave a small laugh. "That I can handle."

"Mainly what I'm trying to get at is that in some ways, even if you live here the rest of your life, you may feel like an outsider. But if you're here a while, most of that will come from inside you."

She thought about that. "You might have a point."

"Maybe." He left it at that.

But he had stirred a memory in her and she recalled a study she had read in one of her psychology courses. "Children who move a lot," she said, "have a tendency not to make the same kind of deep and long-lasting connections that people make when they grow up in one place."

"I know."

"So maybe I can't make deep connections."

"I'm not saying you're broken in some way. If you want to and make the effort, I'm sure you can. Even here, once this mess blows over."

"Why did you bring this up?"

"I was just wondering. I grew up here. The only time I felt like an outsider was when I was away at college, and when I came back I was home. Your experience struck me as different and I wondered how it made you feel."

"Well, now you know."

"And you want to change that."

"You bet I do."

"Then stick around. Don't even think about leaving. It's hard right now, but I can tell you from my own experience, it'll be worth it. Despite the way things look right now, most folks around here are good people."

"I was thinking about that earlier. The way I was welcomed when I got here. I've never before had neighbors I hadn't even met help me move, or bring over meals while I was settling in. That was a wonderful feeling."

"I know, even when you're used to it. They do the same when somebody gets ill."

"Those are the things I need to concentrate on," she said firmly. Then she added, "My hands are getting cold."

"Don't you have gloves?"

"I forgot them. Besides, I don't have any really good ones for here, just some basic, not-too-warm ones I brought with me."

"Let's go inside, then."

In the kitchen, he rinsed out their mugs and put them in the dishwasher. The dishwasher that inevitably reminded him of Martha. Damn. Well, he needed that warning right about now. He needed to get Cassie safely up into one of the bedrooms and close a door firmly between them.

That proved to be easier thought than done. When he turned around, she was slipping off her jacket. The satiny blouse she wore emphasized the way her breasts thrust forward as she held her arms behind her back. And then she shook herself to get the jacket to slide down.

Full breasts, bouncing slightly despite her bra. She seemed unaware that he turned and was looking. The sleeve slipped off one arm and she twisted to tug her jacket around.

Temptation had never come in a lovelier, more enticing package. Her gently rounded shape was generous in all the right places. That little bit of plumpness that she probably hated—the way so many women did—only enticed him more. She would be soft beneath him, curvaceous in his hands. Hips, real hips, not like so many young women who could almost be mistaken for men from behind. His hands imagined how that fullness would feel and he hardened almost between one breath and the next.

He nearly choked with the hunger he felt, the arousal that suddenly pounded through his veins. Who would have thought that watching a woman pull off a jacket could be so erotic? Not he.

Then she turned to hang it over the back of a kitchen chair and he was treated to a full rear view. A rounded butt cased in denim, perfectly shaped. He was losing it.

As if from a distance, almost deafened by the blood hammering in his ears, he heard himself say, "I meant it when I said you're glorious."

Not beautiful, but something far more: glorious.

She turned sharply, surprise on her face. Then he saw her expression melt into one of welcome, her gaze reflecting heat and delight at the same time. And then a flicker of disbelief.

Why she should disbelieve that she was glorious had him beat all to hell, but he was in no mood to question her or discuss it. He chose to respond to her welcome and her heat.

He was through fighting his desire for her.

He was also past finesse. Without a word, he scooped her up in his arms and carried her toward the front stairs.

She gasped. "Linc! You'll hurt yourself."

"Cassie, you seem to have an exaggerated notion of your size." It was true. He was strong, but she didn't feel heavy in his arms. No, she felt good. His breathing grew deeper, his voice thicker, and he managed to say with his last ounce of sanity, "I'm acting like a caveman. Tell me to stop now, before it's too late."

His heart almost stalled as he began climbing the stairs—a wide staircase, thank goodness, unlike many of the older houses around here—and she offered no response.

Then, unmistakably, he heard her giggle softly. "I kind of like troglodytes."

Her answer exploded in his head, filling him with both wonder and a very deep pleasure. Then she lifted her arm and twined it around his neck.

She was his. Just for now, she was his. The heat in him burgeoned, turning to flames that lapped at his every cell.

At the top of the stairs he turned toward his bedroom, the very same room he had used since childhood. He'd never wanted to move into his parents' room. It would have given him no extra space, since all the bedrooms were the same size, and it was loaded with memories. Including Martha, because Martha had taken it over. It had a better view, being on the corner of the house, and she'd even been pushing to have a private bath installed.

He'd considered it, but it didn't get past that before she

left. Since then, the room had been off-limits except when he needed to go in and clean it.

He hesitated a moment, wondering if taking Cassie in there would banish Martha forever, then decided he could find out another time. If there was another time.

Instead he took her to his own room, with its footless queen-size bed, a small desk, a bedside table and a dresser. Furniture, except for the bed, that had been handed down. Only a night-light provided minimal illumination.

He set Cassie down on her feet beside the bed, and bent his head to kiss her. She welcomed him without hesitation, opening her mouth to his, taking his tongue deep inside.

And her curves, ah, her curves. There was nothing to stop him now, and he ran his palms over her, over her shoulder and back, down to that luscious rump, learning every hill and hollow. Rounded softness greeted him.

A soft little moan escaped her, and her hands gripped his shoulders, digging in as if she feared falling. A primitive sense of triumph overtook him as he realized she was his, fully his. She wanted him as much as he wanted her, and he wanted her more than he'd ever wanted anything.

He released her mouth, giving them both a chance to breathe, then dove in again. This time his hands sought other curves. Their tongues dueled in a timeless rhythm as his hand found her breast and squeezed. It was everything he had imagined, full and firm and so damnably cased in clothing.

But as he ran the flat of his hand across the peak of her breast, she arched her hips into his, the message unmistakable. She was ready.

He was, too, but he wanted it to last. He wanted to learn every bit of her landscape, to discover her every secret, to find the promise she offered without even realizing it.

He turned her a bit so that she was bent slightly over his left arm, and tugged her blouse free of the waistband of her jeans. Slipping his hand beneath, he found warm skin softer than satin. She shivered at his touch, and clung harder to his back.

Perfect, he thought. Exquisite. Everything about her, from the scent of her soap and shampoo, to the chocolaty taste that lingered in her mouth. A hint of feminine perfume, and a musky aroma that was strengthening, signaling her need.

He clutched her hip, pressing her side against his throbbing erection for one long, aching moment. Then his hand began to forage along the edge of her bra, seeking treasure.

"Linc..." she gasped, and the sound of her voice pounded in his ears along with the drumbeat of his blood.

Then the phone rang.

# Chapter 7

"Damn!" He swore sharply as the mood shattered like so much spun glass.

Cassie blinked, feeling the desire vanish as if it had been blown away by an internal tornado. "Linc?" she said, her voice a cracked whisper. Coming back to reality proved unexpectedly difficult.

"I'm sorry. It's well past midnight. It must be an emergency."

She nodded, and was touched when he steadied her as she sat on the edge of the bed. The shrilling phone was on the night table, and he snatched it up.

"Linc Blair." He didn't sound very patient. She watched him, still feeling the hunger even though it had been damped almost to quietude by the startling interruption. She hoped it wasn't an emergency, because if he turned and took her into his arms again, she was going to explode like a banked fire that had only been waiting for fresh fuel.

But she saw his posture change. His shoulders dropped a little. "But he's all right?" Then he said, "Thanks for calling." He put the phone down.

He turned, his face an unreadable mask as if he couldn't decide what he felt. "This couldn't have waited until morning? Like there's damn all we can do about it?"

"What happened, Linc?"

"That was Les. James Carney is in the hospital. He tried to kill himself earlier."

"Oh, my God." As the import of his words hit home, nausea rolled through her in waves and she doubled over. "Oh, my God," she whispered. "Oh, my God."

The bed dipped as Linc sat beside her. He wrapped his arms around her and she turned into his embrace. Shock flowed through her in hot and cold waves.

"He's all right," Linc repeated over and over. "He's all right."

"He's alive," she said brokenly, as tears began to flow. "Alive and all right aren't the same."

"I know, Cassie." His murmur was soothing and pained all at once. "But at least there's still a chance to help him."

"Where there's life there's hope?" She repeated the old saw, then gave way to a sob. "Oh, God, Linc, it hurts. It hurts to know how badly he must have suffered. That he would think of this as a solution."

He held her even tighter, rocking her gently, letting her cry it out. The news about James, she realized, had been like a last straw to the stress of the past week. It was all coming out now, her worry for the student, her uneasiness about the attacks against her. But mostly she wept for James. For all she had been through at times, never had she thought that killing herself was her only way out. She couldn't stand to imagine how that youth must be feeling.

Eventually she realized that she had soaked Linc's shirt with her tears. "I'm sorry," she said thickly, trying to pull away and wipe her face. But he wouldn't let her go.

"Don't apologize," was all he said.

She realized he sounded angry. "Are you mad at me?"

"You? No way. But I'm pretty damn angry with some other people right now. Livid."

Anger hadn't come to her yet. Hurt and fear, yes, but not anger. Even some weariness somewhere deep inside, because this wasn't the first time she had encountered depravity in some people. A teacher soon learned how many children were living in terrible circumstances, how many lived daily with fear, poverty and hunger. The secrets they carried and tried so hard to conceal, yet that were written in their behavior and misbehavior even if they denied anything was going on.

But she'd never had a student attempt suicide before.

Guilt slammed her then, overtaking sorrow. Had she somehow been responsible for this because of her intervention? Because she hadn't just walked away after stopping the bullying in the restroom, but had instead caused those four students to get detention?

What she had seen had been bad enough, but had she made it worse? Knowing the way some people thought, it was entirely possible that they'd bullied James even more to make sure he never spoke about what they had done and were doing.

Her stomach grew leaden, and agitation caused her to jump up from the bed and pace the room. Linc reached over to switch on a lamp, probably so she wouldn't stumble against something, but he remained seated on the edge of the bed.

"Do you know how twisted this is?" she demanded.

"What's twisted?" he asked. "Other than the bullying you and James Carney have been getting."

"That I may have made things worse for James by intervening. What do you do when nothing works? It's like being caught in a spiderweb! I try to protect a student, and it only makes it worse?"

"You don't know that," he said quietly. "Cassie, there is no way on earth you can know if you made things worse. What were you supposed to do? Ignore it? Obviously the bullying has been ignored too much and for too long, because it's evidently going on. Without a crackdown, it won't stop. But you can't blame yourself because you did the right thing."

"I can't? Why not? If my action resulted in that boy being bullied even more, why can't I blame myself? God, I feel like a fool. I didn't even pause to consider when I stepped in that I might make it harder on him. I was stupid."

"No."

"No? Of course I was. I saw something and reacted without considering all the possible consequences. I didn't mediate, I just told the four bullies to get to the principal's office."

"Where Les, and you, would have attempted to find out what was behind all this. Mediation. But you didn't get the chance. James even told you to stay out of it."

"He was right. Look what's happened."

Linc rose. "I'm sorry, Cassie, but I don't agree with how you feel. If nobody ever intervenes for fear of making it worse, we'll never stop it. And right now, you don't even know if it got worse. He may have been contemplating suicide for some time, from what his grandmother told you."

"But what made him do it *now?*"

Linc rose, speaking quietly but firmly. "I'm sure as hell going to find out."

"If anyone will talk to you," she said almost bitterly. A sense of responsibility nearly suffocated her. Breathing had become an effort as her chest grew tight and her stomach twisted. "God, I need to do *something!*"

A useless wish, she thought as her mind and body roiled with reaction. It was the middle of the night. What the hell could she possibly *do* right now? As it was, doing something may have made matters worse for a young man.

"I'll get us some coffee," Linc said. "Then we'll go to the hospital. If the family is still there, we can let them know they aren't alone."

Now she felt guilty in another way. "You have a game tomorrow. Today. This afternoon. You need some sleep."

"It won't be my first sleepless night with a game looming. Let's go."

Soon they were driving down the dark tunnel of the endless night again with a couple of travel mugs filled with hot coffee. Cassie's eyes burned, wanting to shed more tears. But along with guilt, anger had begun to grow in her. A terrible anger, as bad as she'd ever felt.

Logically she knew the people involved in bullying James and trying to frighten her were probably a very small number. Most of the people around here, or anywhere, wouldn't do this kind of thing. Most people were actually decent. They might sometimes be unaware, but they weren't deliberately cruel and wouldn't approve of deliberate cruelty.

That was the point of the antibullying campaign, to raise awareness. To make the students understand that it was happening, and sometimes it got far worse than the minor insults most endured. By making them aware of how tolerating even minor bullying could create a climate that allowed it to grow. Consciousness-raising. It worked.

Especially with students of this age, most of whom usually already felt all alone, and if bullied would probably feel ashamed, as if they were somehow responsible. As if something were wrong with *them* and not the bullies. She knew the feeling all too well.

By making more of them aware, they wouldn't feel alone and wouldn't feel that being bullied was their fault. The other hope was to create such an atmosphere of disapproval for bullying that there would be far less of it.

But all of that would come too late for James Carney. Over and over she reran the incident in her mind, trying to figure out what she could have done differently. Because she was absolutely convinced that she hadn't done something she should have.

No, it wasn't a matter of ignoring what those four students had been doing to James. It was a matter of not doing enough of the right thing. Whatever that right thing was.

She almost wanted to hit her head on the window glass beside her, to try to stir up some new thought. But new thoughts proved elusive, and she seemed to be pretty much stuck in an endless loop of guilt, grief and anger with no way out.

Throughout the drive to the hospital, Linc remained silent. She wondered if he was disturbed by her reaction, or angry that he had to make this trip in the middle of the night. Even though he had suggested it, she wouldn't have been surprised if he'd felt he had no choice, given the way she was taking this.

Or maybe he was angry that she hadn't taken this news better and gone ahead with making love to him. Most of the men she had dated—a small enough sample set to be sure—would have been angry about that.

She couldn't ask him, though. Facing her own cowardice, she realized she was afraid of what he might say. What if he thought she was weird, or overreacting, or just a plain nuisance? He wouldn't be the first.

Linc made good time to the hospital. She hadn't noticed that he had driven any faster, but maybe the trip was starting to seem shorter as she got used to it.

As always, he came around to help her out, a gentlemanly courtesy she had thought long dead.

"It'll be okay," he said quietly. "We're going to do something about this, and most people are going to be very upset if they hear about this."

He was probably right. She was sure he was right. But the family's privacy had to be honored as well.

Her nerves tightened as they walked to the waiting room, where an attendant had told them James's family was waiting. Apparently he was not far enough out of the woods that his family was ready to go home.

As the one who may have started this ball rolling with her intervention last week, Cassie wondered what kind of reception she would receive. She wouldn't be able to argue with them if they blamed her, despite what James's grandmother had said.

James's parents, Maureen and Jack Carney, were alone in the waiting room. They held hands, and while Jack appeared angry, Maureen looked more frightened.

Linc made the introductions—he really *did* seem to know everyone. Cassie gathered her courage and asked how James was, hoping she didn't hear…*as if you care.*

"Unconscious," Jack Carney said. He was a slender man who, unlike many of the people in these parts, didn't look as if he spent a lot of time outdoors. "He's alive, but if he doesn't wake up soon they may have to transport him for additional testing for brain damage."

Cassie's legs turned to water. From what Linc had said of Les's call, she had assumed he was awake. Physically fine, if not emotionally or psychologically. Not facing possible brain damage. She nearly collapsed into one of the plastic chairs. "Oh, no," she said weakly.

"It's bad," Jack said. "It's bad. But we're hoping."

"I am so, so sorry."

Linc slowly sat beside her. "Les made it sound as if James was okay now."

"Okay?" Jack spoke bitterly. "He'll never be okay. He's been bullied everywhere he's ever gone to school. I don't know why. Do you know why?"

Cassie had to shake her head. "He struck me as a bright and very nice young man."

"Who knows why bullies pick their victims," Linc said. "I noticed James was quieter than most, but up until just recently, I hadn't thought of him as withdrawn. Just quiet."

"Of course he was quiet," Jack said. "He's been trying to be invisible for years."

Cassie twisted her hands together, torn between sorrow at what that statement revealed, and anger that James's peers had made him feel that way.

"I should have homeschooled him," Maureen said, her voice raw. "I should have taught him myself and kept him away from all that."

"You had a job," Jack said. He lowered his head, his voice growing heavy. "I had no idea it was this bad. He didn't talk about it. Sometimes the only way we found out was when teachers alerted us."

Maureen looked at him. "Remember third grade? We

didn't know anything was wrong. I'll never understand why the teacher didn't mention the bullying until the end of the year. I'd have taken him out of school then if I'd had any idea. Why didn't James tell us?" She ended on a rising note, then quickly put her face in her hands.

In the midst of her own guilt, Cassie felt Maureen's pain like an added spear to her heart. She rose and went to sit by Maureen. She put her hand gently on the woman's shoulder and tried to find suitable words.

"When they're little, kids often don't tell us things because they think we know already. They endow parents with a kind of omniscience, maybe because they've been caught out so many times when they were being secretive. I don't know, I'm not a psychologist. I just know that it's true. And then when they get older… Mrs. Carney, it's even harder when they get older because there's a tendency to assume responsibility when someone hurts us. All too often we think we must be at fault, and we feel ashamed."

Maureen nodded, but Cassie had no idea if she were really hearing. Probably not. There was too much pain, worry and fear right now.

If she, a teacher who barely knew James and saw him only in class for fifty-five minutes a day, felt guilty about this, she didn't even want to imagine how Maureen and Jack must be feeling. As if she could have. The chasm of horror these parents must have felt exceeded anything in her personal experience.

"I was bullied, too," she said finally, hoping to ease Maureen's mind. "I didn't tell anyone. Not a soul."

Now Maureen turned her head. "Really?"

"Really. It's even hard for me to admit it now. And some bullying…well, it's hard to be sure it's bullying. It has a negative impact, but you're just not sure that person was being intentionally mean, or that you didn't misunderstand. Then there's exclusion. A lot of people don't realize, for example, that selecting students and then telling them to pick a team for some kind of competition, whether it's a race or a spelling bee, can be painfully exclusionary. Believe me, I was always the last person picked for a team when there was a race."

"So you're saying it wasn't that he didn't trust us."

That put Cassie on the spot. She didn't know whether James trusted his parents or not. She had no idea of their family dynamics. "Trust," she said finally, "was probably the smallest part of this. It's so hard for youngsters to figure out what's acceptable, what other people know, and whether they deserve something. By the time they get old enough to start sorting through it, it's become a natural part of their lives, miserable as it is."

Maureen nodded. Then she tugged from her husband's grasp and put her face in her hands. "Please," she whispered. "Please let my baby be okay."

It was a long night. Linc went out and returned with some halfway decent coffee for the Carneys. No one spoke much as they waited for news. As the night waned, though, there was no mistaking the rising level of fear in the Carneys.

And in herself, Cassie admitted. If James didn't come through this, she didn't know how she could ever live with herself.

Sitting there with two people who were plumbing the full depths of hell, she was quite sure they would find it harder, if not impossible. Their tension filled the room like a living, breathing beast.

Finally, just before dawn, a smiling doctor appeared.

"James is awake and he seems to be just fine. He's asking for you."

Maureen burst into tears and hugged her husband. Then they jumped up to hurry to their son's side.

But they nearly broke Cassie's heart when they stopped just long enough to thank her and Linc for keeping vigil with them.

She and Linc walked back to his truck. Cassie knew relief lightened her step and probably Linc's as well.

"I'm gonna take you up on that couch," he said as he put the truck in gear. "We need sleep. We can go back out to the ranch later."

The faint lightening of the day showed Cassie her disabled car again, but Beau had scraped the ugly word off her back window. She was glad not to see it.

Inside, though, when Linc started to turn toward the living room, she took his hand and guided him to her bedroom in back. "You'll sleep better in a bed," she said.

Barely pausing to doff jackets and shoes, they tumbled onto the mattress. For long moments Cassie stared at the ceiling, wondering if anything would ever look the same again, but she was just too tired to evaluate anything. Then Linc rolled over and drew her snugly into his arms. With a sigh, she relaxed against him.

"Sleep," he said. "Everything else can wait a couple of hours."

Her eyes fluttered open to the sound of wind keening. Linc was spooned close behind her, an arm around her waist, and she saw the curtained window. God, his embrace felt good. Before she had time to really enjoy it, or wake enough to wonder why the wind was so loud, he spoke.

"That doesn't sound good," he murmured near her ear. "Let me go find out what the weather is."

At that instant, his cell phone rang. He climbed out of bed, pawed in his pockets and pulled out the phone. "Linc Blair." Then he said, "You're kidding. All right. Thanks, Les."

Cassie snapped upright. "Is James okay?"

"It wasn't about James." He stuffed his phone in the pocket of the jeans he still wore. "You're going to get your wish."

He went over to her bedroom window and drew back the curtains. All Cassie could see was whirling white. She leapt up and went to stand beside him. "Snow? Really?"

"Blizzard. The game's been canceled. They're telling everyone to get home and stay home."

Cassie almost clapped her hands in delight. "I love it!"

Linc gave her a smile. "I'm sure you do. It's early for this kind of thing, though. So, my only question to you is, do you want to head out to my place or enjoy your first blizzard from the safety of town?"

"Will it be safe enough out on the roads?"

"For a while. It's going to get worse, but it just started."

She considered. "I like it at the ranch. I'll bet it's beautiful when it snows."

"Well, come with me, then. I have to go take care of my stock."

Of course he did. She felt almost embarrassed not to have realized he was going to have to look after animals in a storm like this. "I'll help," she announced. "Just let me make a quick change, if we have time."

"I'll make some coffee while you do. Then we're off. It may be a little hair-raising to someone who's not used to it, but the roads will be okay for a while. We're going to get twelve or more inches, though, so if you come you're stuck until we get plowed out. You might want to pack some additional things."

Being stuck with him sounded very good indeed. "I'll hurry."

Okay, he'd lost it. Well and truly lost it. Linc couldn't deny it. He'd had the perfect excuse a short while ago to leave Cassie at home and return to the ranch alone. He could have claimed she would be safer or more comfortable in town. From what he'd learned of her over the last week, he was sure she wouldn't have argued with him. And she *would* be safe for the duration of the blizzard. Even the person who had vandalized her car couldn't be crazy enough to pull something in this weather.

But no, he'd offered her a chance to come to the ranch, where they'd surely be snowed in, and he knew where that was going to lead. Last night hadn't eased the ache one bit, but had instead magnified it. It was sitting in his groin like an irritation, and at the back of his mind like a constant unanswered question.

Reminding himself of Martha wasn't helping at all, either. Cassie wasn't Martha, and while she hadn't put any roots down here yet, and she had even mentioned leaving, some part of him had given in to the hope that she would stay. In short, he had stepped off the dangerous cliff without even really noticing.

That made him stupid, he supposed, but it seemed self-evident now that he was willing to run that risk again because he wanted Cassie. He liked Cassie. Day by day she was worming into his life and his heart and he rather liked her there.

The question had changed. Maybe he was rationalizing his own foolishness, but he was now thinking that he owed it to himself to give this a chance.

It was hard, though, not to know if she felt the same. He knew she wanted him, but did she want any more than sex? It was too soon to ask, if he ever could.

It was sure as hell too late now, he thought. One way or another, this thing between them was going to play out unless she skipped town right after the blizzard, and even by then he might have more of his emotions hanging in the breeze than he would have liked.

Hell, he thought. He'd been fighting his attraction to her since she first appeared on his horizon. He'd never had a chance, he supposed. Not against a need this strong. Well, he'd had a chance, but only back when he was keeping her at a distance. From the minute circumstances pushed them together, this had become inevitable.

Just enjoy the weekend, he told himself. Just enjoy it and then deal with the aftermath. He'd survived it once before, so he could do it again. But whatever the cost, some part of him refused to relinquish the hope, and the experience, of Cassie.

Visibility was bad, though not a whiteout, but the snow hadn't begun to stick on the roads. In the deeper grasses across the fields, grasses that cooled down faster, it had begun to cling, frosting plants in little puffs of white.

"It's beautiful," Cassie said. "It's been so long since I saw snow I'd forgotten. It's started to look as if the world is flocked in white."

"It'll be really gorgeous when the storm passes and the sun comes out. Do you remember all the colors you can see in snow?"

"Prism effect. Barely. I do remember once, though, when I was still living up north, when I realized the snow wasn't white. It amazed me how long I'd spent just glancing at it and thinking it was white, but when I paid attention I saw it sparkled with so many different colors."

"Perception is an amazing thing." It was also a safe topic. "I sometimes wonder how much we miss seeing simply because we box and label things in our minds."

"Probably plenty," she agreed.

Right now, though, they were driving in a white-and-gray cocoon. Even his headlights didn't make it sparkle.

"So this is unusual weather?"

"Believe it. I'm not going to say we've never had a blizzard this early in the winter, but they're rare. And to get so much snowfall at once is rare, too. We're in the rain shadow of the mountains, and they wring most of the moisture out of the air before it reaches us."

"Usually," she said.

He laughed. "Yeah, usually."

By the time they reached his house, the storm had really moved in. The wind was whipping the snow hard enough to sting the cheeks, and blowing it in curtains that occasionally parted to give a glimpse of the leaden sky.

As he turned from pulling Cassie's small bag from the truck, he saw her standing with her head tipped back and her tongue out as if she were trying to catch a snowflake. Except these weren't flakes as much as they were ice crystals.

She laughed, a sound that tugged at his heart, then lowered her head and grinned at him. "This is fun."

It struck him then just how different she really was from Martha. Newcomer? Yes. Could possibly decide to leave? Yes. But Martha wouldn't have been enjoying this storm at all. She'd have been griping about all the things she wanted to be doing instead.

Not for the first time in the last two years he wondered how he could have been so blinded by Martha. If he rolled back the movie of his time with her, her demanding nature popped up over and over again. And he'd been too besotted to realize it. The warning signs had been everywhere, that she wouldn't be content to build a life with a teacher and live on a ranch in the middle of nowhere.

Not for the first time he felt a suspicion that she had seen the ranch as a potential cash cow if he would just sell it and move to a life in a faster lane elsewhere. Hell, it had finally become the bottom line to their relationship, the one that ended it.

She certainly never would have claimed standing out here in the wildly blowing snow was fun. No, she'd have been complaining about the cold, the wind, the way the ice crystals stung. She'd have raced inside to get away from it, then moaned how boring it all was.

*Boring* was a word that should have clued him in. Martha had used the word often. He was never bored, and really couldn't grasp people who complained of boredom. There was always something to do, he didn't need to be entertained. Nor did Cassie seem to need constant amusement, either. Admittedly, he hadn't been close with her for long, but her reaction to the storm was proving to be a brightly lighted line of demarcation between her and Martha.

Inside, she continued to smile as she rubbed her hands together to warm them. "What do we need to do with the animals?"

"You don't have to help." Martha had sought every opportunity to avoid pitching in.

"I want to. So what do we need to do?"

"Round them in close. The dogs will do most of the

work, but I've built windbreaks with hay they can huddle behind. I need to make sure they're in the right place and can't wander too far. I still need to do their morning feeding, too."

"So they eat more than grass?"

"They're grazers, yes, but they get supplemental food to make up for any nutritional deficiencies, and right now there's not a whole lot of fresh stuff to graze. The horse stalls will need cleaning as well."

"Let's go, then."

"How about a hot drink first? You haven't eaten, either."

"I'm fine. Don't the animals come first?"

Of course they did, but he was concerned about her, too. On the other hand, it was refreshing that she understood the priorities.

Maybe this mistake wouldn't turn out to be as bad as he had feared.

The dogs made rounding up the sheep and goats easy, Cassie realized. With a few whistles and a couple of commands, they began to push the animals toward the rows of hay that Cassie hadn't really paid attention to before.

Nor had she noticed the fencing with gates that Linc closed behind them to keep them in relatively small pens. Well, why would she have noticed? She didn't understand the purpose of a lot of things out here and hadn't even thought about them until she saw them in use.

The blizzard didn't seem to disturb either the sheep or goats. As soon as they were safely enclosed, they settled down and began pulling at the bales that surrounded them on two sides, dining as if nothing was going on at all. She loved it.

Cleaning the horse stalls strained her muscles in new

ways after Linc showed her how to use the pitchfork and shovel. It took a while, but soon the horses had fresh beds of loose hay, and troughs full of fresh water and feed.

By the time they returned to the house, visibility approached zero. Linc clung to her gloved hand as if he were afraid she would wander off or blow away.

Either option would have been possible, she thought as they trudged across frozen ground that was beginning to be covered by little drifts of snow wherever it was uneven. She could see the house only in snatches until finally it loomed over them, too big to miss.

She paused on the porch to look back over a world that had gone completely white, and could hardly see the barn.

"You're not going to have to go out there again, are you?" she asked Linc. "You could get lost."

"Not until tonight. If worst comes to worst, I made sure the horses can make it until tomorrow. I'd hate to leave them like that, but…" He shrugged, the conclusion obvious.

The change between indoors and out was sharp. Warmth, no wind, relative quiet. She could still hear the wind howling and the windows rattling as strong gusts hit, but it was a different world in here, cozy and protected.

"How are you feeling?" Linc asked. "Still as upset as last night?"

"I'm relieved James is going to be okay. I hope his family gets him some therapy, though."

"And the rest?"

She half shook her head. "I don't know, Linc." She held out her arms as he helped her out of her jacket.

"I need to get you some better gloves," he remarked as he took hers and tucked them into the pockets of her coat before hanging it on a wall peg.

"I can do that on Monday."

"No, I meant I'll dig some out. I've got a few pairs in a box upstairs I just never got around to donating."

An especially strong gust rattled the entire house, and she felt a draft snake past her shoulders. She glanced at Linc, experiencing a twinge of uncertainty.

As their eyes met, the air became instantly charged around them. She could almost feel searing heat leaping from her to him. She felt as if the oxygen had been sucked out of the room. Her heart slammed hard, and then an ache clenched her between her legs.

Everything else vanished but this moment, this man, and an arousal that grabbed her so strongly, so suddenly, it swamped her.

She never knew which of them moved. All of a sudden their bodies met, their arms wrapped around each other, mouths came together in a hungry, devouring kiss.

Nothing in her life prepared her for the firestorm that swept through her with staggering intensity. In an instant she became elemental in her need. The trappings of civilization vanished, except for clothing, which had become a hindrance to escape.

His tongue plunged into her like a spear, commanding, demanding, conquering. She wanted to be conquered. She wanted to brush everything away and get to the most basic coupling possible, because she had wanted it for so long, because she feared something might happen to intervene.

She wanted to *know*.

Apparently he felt it, too, or sensed her impatience. His hands slipped down her back to grasp her rump. She felt the world spin, although her eyes were closed, her mouth coming alive to an erotic awareness she had never before experienced.

Then she was sitting on the counter's edge, her thighs splayed, and he nudged his way between them until their loins met, a hard, welcome pressure. Instinctively she arched toward him, wanting more, and as she did she broke the kiss.

He didn't seem to mind. His mouth found her throat, hot and wet, pulling a groan from her. Her head hit the cabinet above but she scarcely noticed. Instead she lifted her arms, grabbing his shoulders and arching into him even more.

As his hot, wet tongue traced fiery lines along her throat and ear, she felt his hands slip up under her sweater. Roughened hands, feeling cool against her heated skin. Close, but not close enough. She wanted to feel those hands everywhere, and her nipples ached for more intimate touches.

She felt suspended on a tightly drawn wire of anticipation, excited by his touches, aroused to an almost mindless state. It had happened as fast as if someone had touched a match to gasoline, and the explosion of hunger and want in her was beyond anything she had ever imagined.

Every cell in her body seemed to be demanding its due. *Touch me, touch me, touch me!* rang like a pounding refrain, pushing her toward a pinnacle. Need lashed her as sharply as a whip, so strong it almost hurt.

She gasped again as he pulled her sweater over her head, and cold air met her skin. Then she felt her bra release her breasts, a sensation that excited her even more.

At last, his palms brushed across her nipples, taunting and teasing, each touch drawing a helpless moan from between her lips.

It was a nearly silent communion, punctuated only by sighs and moans. Hands and bodies did all the talking. She tugged at his shirt, but a gentle grip of his hands stopped her. A whisper of protest escaped her. She wanted so badly to feel skin on skin.

But he stopped her only so that he could bend his head and draw her nipple deeply into his mouth, sucking with a fervor that caused a deep clenching between her legs. With each draw of his mouth, she wound ever tighter until she felt she might snap.

But she didn't snap. She tightened even more, her thighs clamping hard to his hips, her hands pulling at his shoulders, every movement a plea for more.

He moved to her other breast, sucking so hard it was almost painful. With his hands, he pulled her rump closer to the edge of the counter, closer to his staff, its hardness unconcealed by layers of denim. Feeling his need that way made her soar even higher, made her want even more, and she tried to rock her hips against him, seeking the pressure and friction she needed as her mind plunged downward to that point of contact, making it the center of her universe.

Images popped into her mind, the things she would like to do to him, the ways she would like him to touch her. They added steam to the heat that was already burning her like a torch.

With a groan, he released her breast. Before she could protest, as cold air hit her wet skin causing a delicious shiver, he pulled her up against him. Instinctively she locked her ankles behind his hips, and wrapped her arms around his broad shoulders.

The room spun and she realized dimly that he was carrying her upstairs. Burrowing her face against his neck, she found warm skin, a hint of stubble, and licked him as he had licked her.

A muffled oath escaped him and he quickened his pace up the stairs. His evident eagerness was more fuel for the fire that licked at her every nerve ending.

Finesse didn't exist. As soon as he set her on her feet, they tore at each other's clothing, impatient and eager, not caring if they were rough, or if buttons went flying. They were past even noticing in their need to come together.

The roughness and impatience aroused Cassie even more. She now teetered higher on the mountain than she had ever come before, sensing a nearby cliff-edge where she could tumble fast into the oblivion of release.

It was close, so close, and she didn't want to wait anymore. The fuel of suppressed fantasies over the last few months joined the realization that it was actually happening. An explosion was beginning in her, sweeping her away before its force.

They tumbled onto the bed. There was an awful moment when everything seemed to stop, and she started to open her eyes only to see him rolling protection onto his magnificent staff. That hardness was for her.

Another spear of pleasure arrowed straight to her core, then his hands pushed her legs apart and he was there. Oh, he was there. He touched her with his fingers, stroking that velvety slit once, twice, causing her to shudder with delight and need, and then the wonderful moments when he slid into her warm depths, filling her, answering an ache that could be answered no other way, stretching her and completing her.

He moved. The first thrust drew a cry of ecstasy from her. She rose to meet him, needing every bit of him deep inside her.

Then it happened. Fast. Hot. Hard. She shattered into a

million pieces of pleasure that almost hurt. Moments later she felt him thrust one last time, and with a deep groan joined her in completion.

Linc came back to earth slowly, relishing the womanly curves and softness beneath him. Glorious. Better than glorious. Some little corner of his mind whispered that he'd been too rough, though, and he was almost reluctant to lift his head for fear he would see disappointment or hurt in Cassie's gaze.

So he stayed as he was, propped on his elbows just enough to allow her to breathe, his face buried against her neck and the soft curve of her shoulder as perspiration dried, and then the air whispered coldly across his skin.

Outside, the wind keened even louder, like a reminder that he had to face the world.

Slowly he lifted his head. Her eyes were closed, her face turned a little to one side. Fear spiked him. Had he hurt her?

"Cassie?"

Her head turned slowly and her eyes opened a little. Then a smile dawned on her face, a warm, content and happy smile.

"You okay?" he asked, his heart lifting.

"Never better," she whispered. "Never ever."

"Me, too," he said honestly. Then he remembered necessities. "I need to run to the bathroom. I'll be right back."

Holding the condom in place as he withdrew his softening staff, he was glad to realize he hadn't waited too long. God, he never forgot himself like that.

He tugged a quilt over her so she wouldn't get cold, then raced to the bathroom. He wanted to get back to her, to cuddle with her under the covers, and take the time to learn her as he hadn't in the time just past.

He looked back at himself from the mirror, and realized that he had never looked as satisfied as he did right then. Damn, that had been something.

Grabbing a razor, he quickly scraped away stubble that he was sure must have reddened Cassie's skin, then he hurried back down the hall to his bedroom, buck naked in the house's chilly air, with one thought on his mind: *get back to Cassie.*

He had lost the battle and had little doubt that he was going to pay a heavy price. All that caution about a woman new to the area had burned away in his hunger for her. Even more stupid considering what had happened to her. He wouldn't be able to blame her if she decided she didn't want to live in a county where people would vandalize her car and leave dead animals on her desk. She'd even mentioned leaving, then backed away from it.

But the taste of this experience was likely to stay with her for a long time, and if it turned to aversion she'd pack and go. No argument about how it was only a small number of people would change that. Especially since he couldn't actually prove it wasn't everyone, and she hadn't been here long enough to believe it.

But all those thoughts seemed hardly relevant as he hurried back to her side. He could take it. He'd taken it before, from a woman who'd become a huge part of his life for so long. Cassie had only just started to become a part of his days. Separation would be easier.

Or so he tried to tell himself. Not that anything he told himself would change the fact that he couldn't wait to climb back into that bed with her.

She was lying on her side, back to him as he entered, staring at the window that rattled angrily in the wind. "It's really bad out there," she remarked as his footstep made a floorboard creak.

Why did he feel as if she had withdrawn? She was simply looking toward the window. He strode over and pulled the curtain back. Whiteout.

"I'm going to have the check the animals soon." While he cared about those animals, he felt a surge of resentment that they might need him at this time.

"I know."

Something in the tone of her voice made him pivot and stare at her. "Cassie? What's wrong?"

The corners of her mouth tipped up. "What could possibly be wrong?"

Plenty, he thought. And that was no answer. Another stab of fear lanced him. His stomach sank. But if she wasn't going to talk…well, there was only one way he could think to deal with this, to try to get to whatever was troubling her.

Reaching the bed, he pulled back the quilt, revealing her. She astonished him by instinctively covering herself protectively, and looking embarrassed.

"Don't hide from me, Cassie. Please. Everything about you is beautiful. Sexy. Marvelous."

She looked dubious and didn't relax.

Damn! Without another word, he slid onto the mattress beside her, gently opened her arms and moved her until he had her pinned on her back on the mattress. She was startled but she didn't fight.

"I know I was a Neanderthal just now," he said, sweeping his gaze over her. "I didn't let you know how beautiful you are. Hell, I didn't even do a decent job of learning you. Trust me, Cassie, I've been drooling over you for months."

Still she appeared doubtful. "You could have fooled me."

"It was the main reason I avoided you."

"That doesn't make sense."

"It would if you knew." He bent and dropped a kiss on each breast, realizing he was going to have to fess up and hating to reveal his stupidity once again. She squirmed at the touch of his mouth. So whatever doubts she had, they hadn't quieted her desire. Good. He almost smiled.

But then it was time to talk, much as he hated to hash this over. But while he was hashing, he supposed he could be loving her, too. He sucked her nipple, more gently this time, and felt it harden in his mouth. Had anything ever made him feel so good?

He lifted his head. "I was engaged. I'm surprised you haven't heard about it."

Her eyes widened a bit and she shook her head.

"Martha. Anyway, we were engaged, we'd been together for well over a year, the wedding was two months away, and she delivered her ultimatum."

"Which was?"

"Sell the ranch and leave with her. She couldn't stand this place. She was bored all the time, there wasn't anything to do, she didn't like the animals, she thought… Oh, hell, never mind what she thought. I was a fool not to have guessed what was coming long before it hit."

He scooted down a bit and dropped a kiss on the thatch of hair between her thighs, feeling another shiver run through her.

"Why should you have known?"

"Because the push was there almost from the start. She

wanted me to remodel the house. She wanted a master bed-room with a private bath. She wanted new furniture. She wanted a lot of stuff. In fact, I have a dishwasher because of her. Kind of silly for one guy, don't you think? Anyway, almost from the outset she wanted to change things. If I hadn't been so blinded, I'd have to have seen her constant discontent."

"Maybe she mostly hid it."

He raised his head. "That's a kind thing to say. Well, hindsight *is* twenty-twenty. And I might see things clearer now because of the way she left."

"Entirely possible." She tugged a hand free from his grip and reached down to stroke his hair.

"Anyway, she wasn't from around here. Like you, she moved here for a job. Clearly this wasn't the place for her."

"So you wanted to avoid another outsider?"

"Bingo. I was drawn to you from the instant I saw you, but I kept telling myself that since you'd probably be leaving at the end of the school year, I should just be smart and stay away."

It seemed so incredibly intimate, even to him, to be lying here with his head so close to her most personal places and looking up at her over her body. He liked it a whole lot, and she seemed to be relaxing a bit.

The need was awakening in him again. He licked her in the crease between her thigh and abdomen, and she shivered. "Linc, you are a devil."

A chuckle escaped him. "You love it."

"I can't deny it."

Relief that he'd diverted any continued conversation away from Martha filled him. He didn't want to talk about the past, or about the fear he couldn't quite escape that he would be judged wanting again. That this woman, too, would be unable to tolerate life here. Not now.

Right now he just wanted to sink into her depths, forget all the worries of the past week, forget his fears for her and for the Carney boy, and just focus in this moment with a glorious woman lying in his bed.

He lifted himself a bit and settled between her legs, his face near the apex of her thighs. "If you have any objections to this," he said huskily, "tell me before I offend you."

"No offense. I've never…"

Never? For some odd reason the thought delighted him He couldn't imagine anyone skipping over these honey-blond curls with their musky scent, but it thrilled him to know he could give her something no one ever had before. He eased her legs farther apart, propped himself on his elbows and gently stroked her velvety petals. As shiver after shiver ran through her, he felt his own body pound its way into renewed need.

His fingers traced her soft flesh, avoiding the very seat of her desire, teasing out the moments, loving her growing excitement. Only when her hips arched up in demand did he lower his head and follow his fingers with his tongue.

She tasted as good as her aromas had promised, and with his tongue he explored every nook of her. Soft moans started to escape her, encouraging him to press on, to stiffen his tongue as he slid it inside her and then dragged it up to her swollen nub.

She cried out, but he remained merciless, flicking her with his tongue until her hips rolled like the sea. The sounds of her pleasure fed his own arousal until he felt as if he would explode.

He felt her crest, heard the cry torn from deep within

her. Still he was merciless, lashing her with his tongue until she was panting and ready yet again.

Only then did he grab a foil packet and rise over her, plunging into her until he could plunge no farther. Her legs lifted, trying to lock around his hips, her hands grabbed at his rump, pulling him in, taking him deeper yet.

They rode the rising tide until at last it tossed them dizzy and sated onto a sparkling shore.

# Chapter 8

They rested tangled comfortably together beneath the quilt, her hand on his shoulder, his arms around her. Time passed, quiet except for the wind outside, but finally he stirred.

"This is the best blizzard ever."

She laughed, a delightful sound, easy and free of shadows. "It must be."

"Unfortunately…"

"I know. The poor sheep, goats and dogs are out there."

"You can shower if you like while I take care of them. I doubt I'll be long. Want me to bring you something to eat?" Eating had been overlooked, he suddenly realized, which made him a lousy host.

"I'll get up. I want to help. Besides, being in a blizzard is a rare experience for me. Almost new, even though I can remember some from my childhood."

He enjoyed watching her dress, taking in every graceful movement, drinking in the loveliness that she was concealing with each new piece of clothing. He realized he wouldn't have changed one inch of her.

Then, feeling like a gawping kid, he hastened to conceal his watching by hurrying into his own clothes. "Let me grab some warmer gloves for you."

It gave him an excuse to run down the hall to the bedroom where he had stored so much of his parents' belongings, things he had meant to give to charity but somehow had never managed to part with.

It also gave him an excuse to cool himself down. He couldn't remember ever having been so supercharged with lust for a woman, not even Martha. Ready again so quickly?

It also gave him an excuse to care for Cassie in a small way. Such a little thing to make sure her hands remained warm. He also found a pair of woman's boots—whose? He couldn't seem to remember—and brought them out. He really needed to take this woman shopping for proper winter clothing, he thought, and relished the idea although he wasn't usually fond of shopping.

The boots and gloves fit her well enough and together they stepped out back into a world gone crazy. The wind came so sharply around the corner of the house that she staggered as if from a blow. Only briefly could he make out bits of the hay wall he had built, which he was sure was rapidly disappearing in wind-blown drifts. He also knew in an instant that it was time for wisdom.

"Don't leave the porch," he said. "Stay right here. You could get lost between here and there in fifteen feet and I couldn't promise to find you."

"You can't go out there, either." Her voice rose a little with concern.

"I'll tie myself to the porch. Promise you'll stay here."

"Of course I promise." She looked at him as if she wondered if he thought she was stupid. "I can see how dangerous it is."

"Sorry. I'm just worried. This is a pretty bad whiteout, but I keep a rope in the mudroom just for this."

And if he had known this storm was coming instead of having his head and feelings so wrapped up in Cassie, he'd have strung the rope out and staked it near the fold so he'd have a secure guideline. As it was, if the wind didn't give him a visual break from time to time, he might not reach his animals.

Although he was reasonably certain they were safe, huddled together out of the wind, probably warmed by a layer of snow. Still, he needed to be sure some animal wasn't in distress. He knotted the rope around the porch stanchion then around his waist. Thank God it wasn't that cold, although the wind chill might be deadly.

Then he stepped off the porch into the white and raging storm.

The rat had sickened her, the car had upset and angered her, but now Cassie felt real terror as Linc waded out into that storm. With each step he grew more invisible, and a number of times he vanished completely in whirling snow.

She needed no better object lesson in how dangerous a storm out here could be. There was little to halt the winds in the wide-open spaces once it passed the western mountains. The treeless expanses offered no hindrance to the fury. The blizzards of her childhood had never been this bad. She'd always been able to pretty much see across the street. She had the feeling that if she stepped off the porch, she wouldn't even be able to see her hand in front of her face.

She hoped Linc was dressed warmly enough. In this sheltered part of the porch, it didn't seem very cold until a gust hit her. The wind chill must be fierce, she thought, and he was out there with nothing to protect him but his clothing.

She couldn't remember anyone having mentioned anything about an approaching blizzard, and wondered if this one had somehow managed to come out of nowhere with almost no warning. How likely was that? She didn't know, being new here, and her knowledge of meteorology was limited at best.

She tried to distract herself with random thoughts like these, but failed. Minutes stretched, and along with them her nerves as she waited for Linc. How long would it take? When should she begin to worry? And what should she do if he was gone too long? Follow the rope? She doubted any help could get out here if he got hurt and couldn't get back to the porch.

She closed her eyes, trying to remember the yard between here and the hay. It had been reasonably flat, she thought. Not likely to cause a serious accident. But she couldn't be sure.

Just as she thought she couldn't take it for another minute, the abominable snowman appeared at the bottom of the porch steps. She almost laughed with relief, almost laughed at the way the snow had clung to him, making him even harder to see.

Then he stomped and shook himself, and Linc reappeared with only little bits of snow clinging.

"Everything okay?" she asked.

"Fine." He flashed a smile. "All cuddled up and cozy

under a nice blanket of snow. Did you hear them? A few of them objected to being bothered."

The image made her laugh again, or maybe it was relief leaving her amused. "So they're doing fine but you're not?"

"I'm just cold. That wind is something else." He stepped up beside her. "Let's get inside, warm up and eat. I want to get on with enjoying the best blizzard ever."

The way his blue eyes sparkled at her warmed her all the way to her toes.

*Be careful,* she reminded herself. No man had ever wanted much more than this from her. Not ever.

Between her own experience and what he had told her about his fiancée, she didn't dare think that Linc would be any different. Sexual attraction had pulled them together, but that was hardly enough to make an enduring relationship. He had plenty of reason not to trust her to stay, assuming he even wanted her to, and she had plenty of reason to expect he'd be like everyone else and drop her.

*Just enjoy the weekend for what it was,* she told herself. *One wonderful weekend, nothing more.*

Sunday morning surprised her. When she awoke, she expected to see a world buried in a white blanket. Standing at Linc's bedroom window, however, she saw a world that seemed to have received only a confectioner's sugar dusting.

"Where did it all go?" she asked.

Linc stood beside her and looked out. "It was probably a really dry snow. With all that wind it just kept blowing away until it hit an obstruction and built up. Let's go check the other side of the house."

In a bedroom across the hall, Cassie discovered where the snow was. A huge drift of it had built up alongside the house, reaching almost to the bottom of the second-story window.

"My word!" The sight astonished her. "Does this always happen?"

"Only with high winds and dry snow. This isn't common, though. Usually we get a lot less snow and it's spread over a winter." He laughed quietly. "Sometimes I feel like I shovel the same snow dozens of times."

As he spoke, a gust made snow dance and eddy over the top of the huge drift, sparking little whirlwinds and clouds.

"Could I just climb out the window and slide down it?"

"In your nightgown?"

She turned to him and found his blue eyes sparkling, his face creased with a smile.

"Of course not!"

He laughed. "I wanted to do it when this happened once before. That was so many years ago. I think I was in middle school at the time."

"Did you?"

He shook his head. "Unfortunately from here it looks like it's a solid drift, but it's probably not. First of all, the snow isn't really packed if it's that dry. And secondly, there's probably a pocket where heat from the house has melted it. You could crash right down behind that drift."

"Well, erase that idea."

He laughed again and slipped his arm around her waist, giving her a squeeze. "You're quite an adventurous spirit."

She wondered how to take that. Given that Martha hadn't found it exciting enough here, that might not be a compliment. The thought darkened her mood.

She showered and dressed in jeans and a green hoodie then went down to join him in the kitchen, wondering how this all would end. He had plenty of reason not to trust a woman who had just moved here. She had plenty of reason to expect to be dropped as soon as the sexual heat subsided a little.

They were both fools, she thought wryly, playing with a fire they knew could burn them badly. Wasn't the saying "once burned, twice shy?" Neither of them seemed to have learned that fully.

The kitchen was bright with the morning light. Every now and then a gust of wind moaned around the house, but nothing like the day before. They managed not to get in one another's way as they made a breakfast of toast, scrambled eggs and orange juice, but she noticed that he seemed to have pulled back a little. No touches. No quick little kisses. He had returned to avoiding her. It cast a cloud over an otherwise perfect day.

"I might be able to get you home this afternoon, considering how most of the snow has blown around. The roads are probably pretty clear and I have a plow for the front of my truck."

She looked up from her plate, her mood sinking even more. But before she could respond in any way, he continued.

"I don't really want to take you back. I can't arrange to get your car fixed until tomorrow, so you'd be stuck, and I need to be here later to take care of the animals anyway."

Up and down, a rollercoaster of the heart. He didn't want to take her back, but the reasons had nothing to do with wanting her to stay. Staring at her plate again, she tried to tell herself not to be a fool, not to take everything he said so personally, and for heaven's sake, stop trying to read deep meaning into his every statement. The self-admonishment didn't work.

He spoke again. "We should finish up that bullying presentation."

She still felt deliciously sore and sated from all their lovemaking yesterday and last night, but now he was all business again. It was a pattern she knew too damn well.

"Sure," she said, hoping her voice sounded reasonably normal. Afraid that she might reveal the sorrow that was engulfing her.

God, was she being stupid or what? This man had barely spoken to her for months, and now after little more than a week of working with him and a short period of making love with him, she was this invested?

No way. Not possible. She shoved the sadness from her mind and focused on the really important things, like the antibullying program, like whether they could find out how James Carney was doing, and whether they should include him in their example.

An odd thing happened as they were wrapping up the presentation that afternoon. It was as if her brain had refused to process all that had happened on Friday: the shoving she had endured when they were dancing, the vandalism of her car. Maybe she'd been refusing to accept a lot since she'd found that rat on her desk.

Whatever, a shell seemed to break and it all hit her and hit her hard, as if she'd been living in a fantasy where these things only appeared to be happening. But they were actually happening. Really and truly.

She knew when she went home, whether later today or tomorrow, she was going to be alone with a fear she didn't want to recognize, had indeed been sublimating for the most part.

She had been in some kind of denial, and now denial deserted her.

Breathing became suddenly difficult. She bent over at the table, wrapping her arms around herself, battling down a tide made of equal parts rage and fear.

"Oh, my God," she breathed.

"Cassie? What's wrong?"

"I think…it just hit me. All of it." She had to squeeze the words out as if she were using the last oxygen in the room. Afternoon light was turning golden. The wind still moaned occasionally from outside, but there was no air inside. None. She felt her brain begin to swim.

Linc was suddenly beside her, pressing her shoulders. "Get your head down," he ordered, but gently. "Put it down."

The table was in the way. She felt him turn her chair with surprising strength, then press again until her head met her knees. She gasped for air, feeling her gorge rise at the sickening accumulation of things she had been trying not to think about.

He rubbed her back as she remained bowed over. "I wondered," he said. "You were entirely too calm on Friday. I wondered when this was going to hit you."

She couldn't believe it had taken this long. Memories surged, filling her mind's eye. The rat. The Carney family at the hospital, her car, the confrontations, even that phone call. One thing she knew for sure was that she didn't feel safe. No, she was scared. Everything that had happened was such an overreaction to detentions that at last it really began to terrify her.

Whoever was behind some of this was unhinged.

"Oh, God," she whispered. "He's sick!"

"Sick?" He was still rubbing her back gently. "The guy who vandalized your car?"

"And killed that rat."

He was silent a for a few seconds, then pulled a chair over so that he sat beside her. He resumed rubbing her back gently. "It did cross my mind," he admitted. "It's so out of proportion."

At last she was able to suck in a full lungful of air and then another. But the sick feeling and the fear hadn't fled.

She straightened slowly, realizing that her world had altered yet again. Making love with Linc, discovering so much passion and delight, had been an earthquake by itself. But now she was having another one.

"I think," she said slowly, "that I've been trying to put it in the category of stupid pranks." Her gaze tracked to him. "All of a sudden I can't do that anymore. Tell me I'm overreacting."

He hesitated visibly. "I can't do that. I wish I could. But even if there's only the merest possibility—and I admit it crossed my mind—it would be really stupid not to be cautious. That's why I didn't want you to be alone. Partly because I was worried about when this would hit you, and partly because I can't be a hundred percent certain it's not going to escalate."

"Then why did you suggest taking me home?"

"Because you have a right to make your own decisions. If you wanted to get home, I'd take you."

She closed her eyes, trying to absorb what felt like a series of blows: realizing that all that stuff last week had been real, that her car was still sitting in her driveway with flat tires, one of which had been punctured, that there really had been a butchered rat on her desk, that a lot of people seemed to be angry with her for turning over the rock under which bullies hid…and that Linc's sole reason for bringing her out here this weekend was protective.

Man. Had she been using his attention as a distraction?

Or had she been totally distracted by his attention? And how could she have so minimized the threatening actions against her? The flickers of fear that had penetrated before were nothing like the full-scale epic of horror and guilt she was feeling right now.

"Cassie?"

It was a question of some sort, but he didn't say what he wanted to know. Maybe it was just a check to see if she were still alive and breathing. Which seemed to be the main part of his interest in her.

He'd offered to take her home, saying it had to be her decision. Nice, except now she was wondering if he thought she hadn't liked his lovemaking and just wanted to get out of here. Or if he was looking for nice ways to get rid of her.

On top of everything else that had just come home in a gut way, she felt too confused to sort anything out. Someone wanted to hurt her. Of that she was now fairly certain. But there was no way to know how far he or she might go. Maybe they just wanted her to quit and leave town. Maybe it would stop there. Or maybe they had some kind of real grudge she couldn't begin to imagine.

"Damn it!" The words exploded out of her as everything coalesced into anger. Anger at least wasn't confused and she almost welcomed it. Rising, she hugged herself and started to pace the length of the kitchen.

"What?" he asked.

"Do you even need me to explain?"

"Probably not," he admitted, "but you might as well get it all out. It usually feels better."

"That depends on how I get it out. Something like this creep is doing..." She let go of that thought, focusing instead on something else.

"Okay, I'm scared. It might not stop with the car. Best

case, this creep leaves me alone, having made his statement of disapproval. Or maybe because word of James's suicide attempt is probably getting around. You'd have to be a cretin not to climb back under your rock in the face of that."

"You'd think."

"Assuming, of course, that people know it might have been associated with him being bullied."

"We know it was. His family knows. They've certainly been talking, and we're going to talk about it at the assembly."

"But that assumes whoever is trying to get me to quit and leave town hasn't got some other axe to grind. Or isn't just out-of-control nuts. And frankly, reacting this way to detentions is so over-the-top. That's what's scaring me. Even one of the student's own mothers just wanted to defend her son. All she did was confront me in the parking lot and insist her son couldn't have done anything wrong. I've faced that before, I'll face it again. That's within the realm of normal reaction. Even the pushing while we were dancing. That was just some people who wanted me to be aware they didn't think that was enough to merit action. I don't think it's associated with the other stuff at all, like the phone call, or the rat and my car. Those exceed a typical response."

"I agree," he said quietly.

She paused her pacing and looked at him. Why did he have to be so gorgeous that she kept wanting to forget everything else? "What you said about the basketball championship. Could somebody really get this heated over something like that?"

"Heated, yes. Enough to make you feel threatened? Not most people."

She nodded. "I agree. But I don't have the pulse of this place the way you do."

"Well," he said dryly, "I do believe most of us left the Wild West and showdowns at high noon behind us."

That caused her a pang. "I wasn't trying to insult your neighbors. It's just that last week you said…"

"I know what I said. I was trying to explain why people might be upset that a star basketball player could be unable to play if he gets another detention. What I said about the rat…" He shook his head. "Cassie, I wasn't trying to minimize it, not really. Yes, kids here are more used to that kind of thing because of hunting and ranching, but to do something like that to send a message…" Again he shook his head. "I just didn't want you worrying needlessly if that was the end of it. Clearly that's not the end."

"So you were just trying to reassure me?"

"Yeah. I was worried about it at the time, and I'm still worried."

"I'm a big girl," she said sharply. "Don't try to shield me or brush things off."

"I'm sorry."

But she didn't want him to be sorry. He was a naturally protective man as she had learned this past week. It had probably been instinctive for him to not want her to get too upset without further cause. "Don't apologize. Just don't do it again."

"Fair enough. So where does this get us? Are you going to pack and leave for other parts?"

"No." Of that much she was certain. She might be frightened of where this could go. Clearly she was the target of someone who was angry with her. But how much of a threat was he? She fought to tamp down the morass of fear that tried to rise again.

Slowly she returned to the table and sat. "I'm mad. I'm stubborn. I'm not going to be pushed around by some coward who makes anonymous phone calls, slashes my tires and uses a dead rat to get his point across. What's more, I was really starting to like this town."

"And?" he asked.

"I'm staying. I'm going to ride it out. I'm not going to turn tail."

"It could get dangerous. I can't promise you it won't. Not after two very obvious threats of violence, that rat and your car."

"They're probably just threats," she said decisively. "But even if they aren't I'm staying. I'm going to keep working to put an end to bullying, and to teach my students the best that I can. I absolutely refuse to give in to a bully, and that's what this guy is."

"Then you'd better get ready to have me around a lot until we're sure this is over."

"I can deal with that." Which was a rather offhand way of skirting the truth: she *wanted* him around. Giving herself an inward shake, she told herself to focus on work, on her job, on her students. It had saved her before.

## Chapter 9

They made love again that night, but only once. Cassie didn't know if she imagined that Linc seemed a little withdrawn, but she knew she was tightening into her protective shell again. The passion filled her with melancholy even as it carried her to heights of delight. Barriers that were at least partly hers, and perhaps partly his, seemed to be rising again.

The feeling stayed with her as he took her home in the morning, as he called his friend to come take care of her car while she prepared for school. The magic of Saturday seemed to be waning.

All to the good, she told herself, even as she began to realize that brave words spoken in the shelter of Linc's ranch seemed almost foolhardy now that she was faced with returning to school.

For the first time she felt honestly nervous about going to work, about facing her classes. So far her students didn't seem to have joined the anti-Cassie camp, but what if the antipathy she had experienced on Friday had now reached them? What if she looked into hostile faces?

She'd deal with it, she promised herself. She'd deal with it the way she had dealt with so many things in her life: by ignoring it until it went away. Often that was the only option.

Her first indication of a sea change came from the mechanic Linc had called. When she tried to give him her credit card for the tow he waved it aside.

"No charge for any of this, Ms. Greaves," he said. "Wouldn't want you to think that folks around here would approve of whoever did this."

"But…" Even as her heart swelled with appreciation, she felt guilty. "You need to make a living, too, Morris."

"I'll make one even if I do this. Put that card away."

She was sure her mouth didn't close until her car disappeared down the street on the back of the truck.

"Wow," she said finally.

"Plenty of generous people in the world," Linc remarked. "The ugly ones seem to get the most attention, though."

She couldn't argue with that. The next sign of a shift came before her first class. Les came looking for her, and he was beaming. "You'll never guess what's going on."

"What?"

"Some townspeople, mostly parents, are setting up a fund to help James Carney's family with medical bills and counseling costs. And what's more, the school email and voice mail is full of requests for a special evening assembly for parents to discuss bullying."

"That's wonderful!"

"I told you an assembly was the best way to handle this.

Now we'll get the parents involved. I hardly dared hope we'd get such a response."

"We might not have," she reminded him. "Except for James. Have you heard anything? Linc and I were at the hospital Friday until he was out of danger, but I haven't heard since."

"I called his mother this morning. He should be released today, but she's not planning to bring him back to school." Les sighed, a frown settling over his round face. "She said it was just until he had some counseling, but I don't know, Cassie. This was a terrible thing. People are responding positively, but that doesn't mean we can change the culture overnight."

"I'm sure we can't. But this is a giant step."

A giant step that brightened her morning considerably, as did the students in her classes, who seemed to want to do something, whether it was sending some kind of message to James and his family, or taking on the bullies in their midst. Suddenly it seemed too long to wait until the Friday assembly. Everyone wanted to do something constructive *now*.

Behind that, though, she sensed something else, a kind of uneasiness. It came, she thought, from awareness of their own past transgressions, from the near loss of someone their own age. From guilt and awareness of mortality. Not knowing what else to do, she put her lesson plans aside for the day and just let the students talk, making a mental note that they might need to get the school psychologist in on this.

The day became emotionally exhausting for her as she tried to guide students through their mixture of feelings. Some started out tough, insisting they would never kill themselves over anything as stupid as bullying. Some spoke about how they had been bullied and how it had made them feel. In class after class, a slow consensus was reached: bullying was a bad thing.

She suspected the conversation would go on for days, and she was determined to have it if that was what the students wanted. So she gave them the situation: if they wanted to continue the discussion, they'd have to make up time on the lessons. They voted to make up the work with very few dissenters.

Having allowed them to choose, she was quite certain they would do so. At the end of the day, she was feeling a whole lot better about everything, and already figuring out how to alter her lesson plans for the makeup without pushing the students too hard to keep up.

"Ready to go, Teach?"

She looked up and saw Linc framed in the doorway, his jacket hanging open, his backpack slung over one shoulder.

"It's been a good day," she said as she gathered her last few things.

"You, too? We talked about bullying all day."

Her heart lifted and she returned his smile. "Yes." Then her smile faded. "Why does it always take a martyr to get a point across?"

"People can ignore a lot until they get jolted out of their ruts. How else could we survive?"

That was an excellent point. Walking with him across the parking lot as the afternoon faded rapidly toward twilight, she tried to tell herself not to expect too much, that it would take a long time to really change anything, that after the shock passed it would be easy to forget. "Shock works just so long."

"I know," he said as he opened the truck's door for

her. "That's why I didn't ignore it today. Strike while the iron's hot."

She slid into the seat. "Don't you have a practice?"

"Canceled. We're going to be playing a makeup for the game Saturday. I'll have to get back here by six and we'll play at seven."

"On a school night?"

"Yeah. Only way to prevent messing up the season schedule. Want to come?" he asked as he pulled the truck onto the road.

Since she was feeling considerably better today than yesterday, she actually had to think about it. A football game would be fun, but she had to rework all those lesson plans. And when she tested the sore space inside, the place left by the events of the past couple of weeks, she found it wasn't terribly tender. Her faith had been restored, and she was inclined to figure that nothing would happen that she couldn't handle.

"I need to work on lesson plans," she said. "We're going to get into a real mess with the syllabus if I don't figure out how to space things so the students don't get overwhelmed. I'd better just stay home and work."

"Not afraid?"

She glanced his way and smiled slowly. "Actually, no. Like I said yesterday, whoever did those things is a bully and a coward."

"And today you believe it?"

"Actually, I do. It was like everything changed today. Peoples' opinions seem to have swung around. The bully will probably crawl back under his rock now that people aren't upset."

He was silent as he steered them around a corner. "Probably." He spoke the word slowly. "I don't know, Cassie. I wouldn't have expected anyone to vandalize your car, or put a rat on your desk. Someone has a kink."

"Obviously. Are you trying to frighten me?"

His head shake was quick and certain. "No. I just want you to be cautious. People around here may be experiencing a shift in opinion, but that doesn't mean he has."

She couldn't argue with that, but she felt more confident than she had since this whole affair had started. And despite her burst of fear yesterday, she had begun to realize that the thing she most needed to do for herself was stand up. If she had begun to lose sight of that, her students today had definitely reminded her. They needed her, and other teachers, to help them work through this, and they had shown good hearts for the most part. Turn tail now? No way.

"None of it hurt *me,*" she reminded him, and maybe herself. "All of it was done in a way that would seem to indicate the bully doesn't want to be identified."

She gasped with surprise as they came around the corner. Her car was sitting in the driveway, and it sparkled. "Oh, my! Morris even washed it!"

Linc chuckled quietly. "I told you most people around here are good folks."

He pulled in behind her car, and she grabbed her backpack and climbed out before he could assist her. She walked around her compact and peered inside. "He even vacuumed it! My word!" She touched it. "I'd forgotten it could look this good."

"The key is probably under your doormat," Linc said.

She checked immediately and was relieved to find it. Any mischief-maker could have helped himself if that was a custom around here. Finding the key reassured her even more.

Linc came inside with her. She dropped her bag on the battered couch and faced him, smiling. "It's amazing how fast things can change."

"We've seen a really huge swing since you found those boys bullying James," he agreed. "First all the way down and then up."

"What can I do to thank the mechanic?" she asked him, still thinking about the loving care he'd bestowed on her car for free. "That was really above and beyond. A bottle of wine?"

"Beer would probably go over better. I think he'd appreciate the gesture."

"That's what I'll do, then." Feeling ever so much better, she spun in a little circle. "I can't believe that yesterday I felt like everything was crashing down on me. A weight is gone."

She noticed, however, that he didn't appear quite as thrilled as she was feeling. She glanced away, wondering if she had overreacted yesterday or if she was overreacting now. Yesterday she had been seriously frightened, wondering what kind of attack would come next. Then she had decided that whoever had been bothering her really hadn't done all that much, and what he had done indicated that he was a typical bully, a coward.

She still believed that. Whoever had butchered the rat and vandalized her car had wanted to frighten her, but he hadn't had the gumption to face her directly.

"Do you think I'm being foolish?" she asked finally.

"No." He stepped toward her and surprised her by wrapping her in his arms and hugging her close. It felt so good to be near to him again, to feel as if he weren't holding her at a distance. Last night's feeling that he was drawing away had lingered throughout the day, a subtle sort of ache, a sense of impending loss like a backdrop to all the good things that had happened since this morning. Part of her wanted to pull away, but another part of her took charge and she returned his hug.

"I understand," he said, "that yesterday it all crashed down on you. I'm not quite as sanguine that this bully will settle down now that public opinion is starting to rise against bullying. But maybe you're right. So far he's been a coward, that's for sure. Trying to frighten you without facing you. Typical of bullies."

"Exactly." Reluctantly she stepped back, reminding herself that she shouldn't get in any deeper. He had his reasons for fearing involvement; if there was ever a woman made to fit the bill of what worried him, it was her. She'd been here only a few months, she might decide not to stay.

Her own fault, too, because she could clearly hear herself saying more than once that she should resign and leave. After the rat, especially, she'd been unnerved enough to think about it seriously.

Equally important was that she was certain he had only spent so much time with her because he felt he needed to protect her and reassure her. He seemed like that kind of man, and the sexual attraction…well, little could be built on that. It flared, but it always quieted. She had enough married friends to have observed that.

So they'd been overcome, but that didn't mean she had to put her heart at his feet. Asking to get trampled once again, and this time by a man who had good reason not to trust her, didn't seem bright. If the background ache she'd been feeling was any indication, she was already in too deep. Definitely time to step back.

"Want something to eat?" she asked brightly without quite looking at him. "You've got to eat before the game."

Linc felt her pull away, saw how she avoided his gaze, and wondered what the hell he'd done wrong. Then it struck him: she was pulling away because she no longer felt she needed him.

Why should that be such a shock? Martha hadn't needed him enough to stay. Cassie had needed him since the day when that rat showed up on her desk, understandably. She was a newcomer around here without resources of her own yet. He had stepped up like some kind of hero and she'd welcomed the support and the protection he'd offered.

But now she felt everything was going to be okay. He believed the passion they had shared had been real, but beyond that? Beyond that there was evidently nothing.

He'd been a fool once again. His stomach turned to lead and his mouth soured. Another Martha? Maybe just a different version. But why should he be surprised? Why would any woman who hadn't grown up here want to hitch her wagon to a man who was just a teacher and part-time rancher. There were certainly better prospects out there, even around here.

"No thanks," he said. "I've got something back at the school. Maybe I'll stop by for a few minutes after the game. If anything disturbs you, I'll have my cell phone on, but I might not be able to hear it during the game." He started toward the door, then hesitated, his conscience plaguing him.

"Cassie? Are you sure you don't want to come to the school?"

She shook her head. He wondered why her face suddenly looked a little…wooden? Sad? He couldn't quite read it.

"Thanks," she said, giving him a small smile. "I'll be fine."

He walked out, feeling as if he had just missed something very momentous.

Wishful thinking, he told himself. That's all it was. At some level he'd dared to believe Cassie was different from Martha.

Evidently not.

Some unspoken conversation had just been had, but Cassie was only sure of her part in it. She had pulled back, yes, but she had offered him a meal, something far less dangerous than where that hug could have led. Then he had seemed to want to get out of there as fast as possible.

Mine fields, she thought. They were both full of them. She didn't trust him because he didn't trust her. He had plenty of reason not to trust her, and she had plenty of experience to tell her that trusting a man too quickly led to grief.

An aching sense of fatigue washed through her. Did she really want all this complexity? Not that it appeared she was going to have much choice. She'd pulled back, he'd left. They were quickly crawling back into their safe little shells.

Early twilight was claiming the world and darkening her house. She looked out the front window, saw the streetlights start to wink on from farther down the street. Surprisingly little snow had caught in her front yard, and the sidewalks and driveway were clear. The wind… Remembering the drift outside Linc's house, she walked around, turning on lights for comfort, and looking out windows to see where the snow had ended up.

Mostly in her backyard, she realized. Opening the back door and looking out the storm door, she realized she wouldn't be able to open it. Because of the other houses around, the drift didn't reach her second floor, but it came halfway up the door. From there she could see that most of the snow in this neighborhood had wound up behind and between houses. The street was swept clean, but everything else was buried.

Well, good to know, she thought, that she had only one way out and that was through the front door. She glanced at the clock, saw it was still plenty early, not quite dinnertime, so she pulled out her computer, looked up James's home number and called. His mother answered.

"Hi, Mrs. Carney, it's Cassie Greaves, James's math teacher. How is he doing?"

"Much better than he was. I'm going to be homeschooling him, though."

Cassie didn't argue. There was no good argument. "Is he well enough to see me? And if you want me to, I'd be glad to tutor him at home in math."

There was a definite hesitation, then Maureen's voice thawed a bit. "That would be helpful. I'm rusty on some things."

"Aren't we all?"

"You come over," she said. "You tried to protect him. Might do him some good."

Cassie felt another pang of guilt, as aware as anyone that she might have caused the bullying to worsen by her intervention.

Struggling with the guilt, she grabbed her things and a book she thought James might like to read. Outside, the setting sun outlined the western mountains in fiery red. It almost looked like the sky was on fire.

She was glad she didn't believe in omens.

James and his parents lived in a neat, small house in a neighborhood that looked like it had been built right after the Second World War. Cassie hiked up the drive, feeling the wind cut at her cheeks and try to snake into her jacket.

Maureen Carney opened the door, and greeted her with a tired but honest smile. "Come in, Ms. Greaves. James is in the living room, but I honestly can't tell you how he's feeling. He's been awfully quiet."

Cassie stepped in, noting that the house offered only the smallest of foyers, just enough to step inside and doff a jacket before reaching the doorways that opened off either side.

"James," Maureen called, striving for brightness, "Ms. Greaves is here." No voice answered her, but the woman continued to smile wanly and led Cassie into the living room.

James, looking even smaller than he had before, lay on the couch. He wore a green sweatshirt, and a ripple afghan covered his legs. There was something on the TV, but the volume was low, as if he wasn't really paying attention.

He looked awful. His eyes were sunken, and every line of his face seemed to drag downward. His dark eyes fastened to her, but only briefly.

"Hi, James," she said quietly. "I wanted to see how you're doing. Your fellow students are very upset about you. We talked about it all day."

He hunched his shoulder, as if trying to pull away, but he didn't answer. Cassie sat on an armchair facing him, wishing she knew the right words. Finally, she pulled out the book and leaned forward to place it on his lap.

"I think you'll like it, since you're so good at math. It's full of amusing stories about some great mathematicians."

"Doesn't matter," he said finally in a muffled voice.

She hesitated. Then, firmly, she announced, "It matters. *You* matter. I've seen some real talent in you, and you probably have a lot of talents you haven't even discovered yet. You have a lot to offer the world."

"You wouldn't know."

"Actually, yes, I would. I've been bullied, you know. It made me doubt myself and feel ugly and utterly alone. But here I am, trying to make a difference by teaching. One thing I know for sure, sometimes the biggest contribution any of us makes is a smile and a kind word. You're perfectly capable of that. Don't take your smile away from someone who might need it."

His eyes flickered toward her, then fell away. At least he was starting to hear.

"Your mom says you won't be coming back to school. I'm sorry to hear that, but I understand. I told her I'd be happy to tutor you in math if you like."

"I don't know," he said heavily.

"It's early days," she answered and looked at his mother. The woman was standing out of his line of sight, and right now she looked haggard as she stared at her son. Guilt. How much more guilt must she be feeling than even Cassie? How many times had she hoped her son was silent because the bullying had stopped? How many times had she told herself, and him, that it would stop eventually? And now this, the most desperate cry for help anyone could make, one of utter hopelessness.

She returned her attention to James and decided to take the bull by the horns. "Did the bullying get worse after I stepped in? Because if it did, I am so very sorry."

Now he stared at her. "It never stopped. Never. Like you hadn't done anything. They didn't hit me again, but they didn't leave me alone. They said they were going to get me when they were away from the school."

"Did they?"

"Not really. But they started a page online to slam me. A bunch of people joined in."

Cassie drew a sharp breath and wondered why she hadn't thought about the potential impact of social networking. God, how could she have overlooked that? "How did you find out about it?"

"There was a note in my locker. I didn't want to look, but I did."

She nodded. "I wish I'd looked into that."

"You wouldn't have found it. They didn't use my name or anything on the page. But everyone knew. Everyone was talking about it." His voice, which had been growing stronger, began to fade again. "I'm tired."

"Of course you are. You've been through hell." She didn't think this was a good time to pull punches. "I'll leave you now. But I want you to know I'm very sorry if I made it worse for you, James. But I couldn't ignore what I saw in that washroom."

He turned his face away. "I know. I guess I'm okay with it. You at least tried to do something. You're the first one."

Cassie heard his mother gasp and found Mrs. Carney looked horrified, with a fist to her mouth as if she were trying to hold in a cry.

"I'll come back in a few days," she said, rising.

He didn't answer.

Cassie grabbed her jacket in the foyer and stepped out onto the front porch. Without another word, Maureen closed the door behind her.

Determination grew in her all the way back home. Tomorrow she would address the matter of that social networking page with Les. It didn't matter if it was all happening outside of school. There had to be some way to stop it. But she couldn't imagine what. A sense of helplessness hit her as she pulled into her driveway and parked, a help-lessness so strong she wanted to pound her steering wheel.

Frustrated but determined to at least bring up the issue, she gathered her purse and climbed out of the car. It wasn't terribly late yet, still plenty of time to work on revising her lesson plans. She had to get that done before everything went off the rails.

She wondered how the game was going. She could hear sounds from the direction of the stadium, indicating that a lot of people had come out for the game, cold notwith-standing.

She was on her front step when she remembered she hadn't gone grocery shopping. A glance at her watch told her she had just enough time to at least grab something for tonight and the morning.

She tried not to think about Linc as she climbed back in her car to make the short run. She didn't want to imagine how he looked there on the sidelines coaching the team. She didn't want to imagine that he looked at his cell fre-quently to see if she had called.

She didn't want to imagine him at all, but there he was, popping up anyway. Maybe instead of working on her les-son plans, she ought to dally in the grocery until closing time. Linc would probably be wrapping up the game by then. Then she wouldn't have to waste her planning time by mooning around the house wondering if he'd drop by. The wait would be short by then. If he came.

Dang, she was a fool. Wasting all this time thinking about a man who didn't deserve it if only because he wasn't interested in the long term.

Let it be, she told herself. Let it be. Focus on work. Focus on the bullying program. Focus on the important stuff that she could actually do something about.

But why then did Linc seem as important as all the rest of it? That was the way to pain.

Memories from the past week, and most especially the weekend, insisted on distracting her from the routine chore of grocery shopping. She wasn't apt to get much work done this way.

Sighing, she finally completed her shopping and headed home. She wondered if ever before in her life had her thinking been so scattered and ungovernable. Even to herself she didn't seem to be making sense.

At home she grabbed her grocery bags and headed inside, wondering if a cup of coffee might help her gather the tattered ends of thought and focus.

But as she was emptying the bags, she heard a sound. In an instant her thoughts stopped hopping around and focused intently.

She was not alone.


The itch to get back to Cassie grew more and more overwhelming as time ticked by and Linc kept checking the game clock. At the final two-minute warning, he almost dumped everything on his assistant coach and took off.

All his resolutions not to get involved again, especially with a woman who might move on, had evaporated. And he knew just the moment they had evaporated. When she had pulled back from him, as if to place a distance between them.

He knew he was at least partially responsible for that, and as the evening passed, the need to talk to her increased until it became almost unbearable. He wanted to find out what exactly was causing this sense of distance. He wanted to clear the air, and unless she had discovered she wasn't interested in him, he wanted to tell her that he was willing to take the risk.

Hell, as he tried to keep his focus on coaching, his thoughts kept running to her. Willing to take the risk? Damn, he'd already taken it. Leapt into the fire with both feet.

And now he couldn't simply walk away.

He was troubled, too, by her being alone. Everything she had said about the person who had come after her made sense. The guy—at least he assumed it was guy—clearly was a coward and a bully, unlikely to go beyond anonymous threats.

Unfortunately, whether it was sensible or not, he didn't quite believe it. In fact, the more he thought about all that had happened that day, the more uneasy he got. What if this guy was pushed by the groundswell of support for Cassie and James Carney? What if he felt he was the only one left who would take action in his cause, whatever it was?

Did it even matter why? The threats of violence had been implicit, and sometimes people moved beyond threats to action when they felt pushed.

He should never have left her alone. He should have insisted she come to the game with him. Instead of backing away because she had seemed to want him to, he should have pressed the issue, become a caveman if necessary.

The penalty whistle blew and stopped the game again. He ground his teeth. He was probably overreacting, but he felt strongly that he didn't want Cassie to be alone until they could at least be certain this bully had quit. And he felt equally strongly that they needed to talk.

His insecurity combined with hers might be walking

them both in entirely the wrong direction. Or not. What if she told him to get lost? Well, he'd survived it before.

What was killing him as much as anything was the distinct feeling that he shouldn't have left her alone.

Damn it! He turned to the assistant coach, his mind made up.

Cassie stood frozen, facing the counter and grocery bags, listening intently, acutely aware that there was only one way out of this house because of the snow. The front door.

But perhaps she was mistaken. Straining her ears, she heard nothing. No sound, no movement. A faint rumble that she knew to be the forced-air heater in the basement.

Maybe she'd been mistaken. Maybe a temperature change had caused the house to settle a bit.

But she didn't believe it. The hair on the back of her neck was standing on end with the certainty that she was *not* alone.

Okay, she thought. Okay. Whether she was right or not, the sensible thing to do would be to get out of here. Just grab her keys, her purse, her jacket, like she was going out to get something from the car, and get out of here. Maybe pick up her cell phone and call the cops as she did so?

She uttered a small oath as if she were frustrated, and reached for her keys lying next to her purse on the counter. Her cell phone was in her pocket and she stuffed her hand in to grab it. Just in case, she told herself. Forget the jacket. Just get out the door.

She turned and had taken two steps toward the hallway when the man appeared. Aghast, she instinctively stepped back. He was big, very tall and massive. He wore winter outerwear and a black balaclava completely concealed his face and nose. She wouldn't have known who he was even if she had met him before. He stood between her and her only exit.

"Who are you? What do you want?" The questions escaped her instinctively, even as she backed up another step and her mind ran frantically around wondering what she could use to protect herself. Little enough. Her knives were in a drawer, her heavy pans were in a cupboard. Defend herself with a cloth grocery sack?

"I told you to leave."

It was the voice from the phone call. Maybe. She couldn't be sure of that, and she didn't recognize it otherwise. Her heart hammered so hard that breathing had become nearly impossible. Her mouth grew so dry she could barely speak. "Why?" It was a bare whisper. "I haven't done anything to you."

"You're messing with things you shouldn't oughtta. Upsetting folks. Hurting kids."

"But… Was your son one of those on detention?" A little strength was coming back when he didn't outright attack.

"No."

"Then what?" Desperation filled her, even as a voice kept telling her to remain calm, that he hadn't attacked her yet, that maybe he only intended to frighten her. He was certainly succeeding. *Try to talk him down.* "What have I done?"

When he didn't answer, her fear ratcheted up even more, something she wouldn't have believed possible only a little while ago.

She spread her hands along the counter, trying to look casual, but feeling slowly for the drawer where she kept her knives, never taking her eyes off of him.

He stepped toward her and she froze. "You don't get it," he said. "You had a chance to leave and you didn't."

"But what did I do?"

"You know."

"I don't!" Her fingers closed on the drawer pull. "Did you put that rat on my desk?"

An ugly laugh escaped him. "Bet that shook you."

"It did," she admitted, hoping that agreeing with him would calm him. "It made me sick."

"Good. You shoulda quit then."

Bully, she reminded herself. He was a bully. Even now he wouldn't reveal his face. That must mean all he wanted to do was scare her.

She gauged the distance to the door and his bulk between her and it. If she could get him to move just a little more to the side…

She shifted toward the back door. He instinctively sidestepped that way but shook his head. "You can't get out that way."

So he'd checked it all out. He knew she had only one way to go.

"I'll leave," she said. "Just let me go and I'll get in my car and never come back."

"That chance is gone."

Gone? What did he mean? Then she knew. He wasn't here just to scare her. He meant to hurt her.

As that certainty filled her, extreme clarity settled over her. She could either stand here and take whatever he dished out, or she could do everything in her power to fight him.

Should she grab a knife or try to dart by him? She couldn't tell if he had a weapon, although that probably didn't matter as big as he was. Wrenching the drawer pull, she yanked it open and felt for her big chef's knife. She gripped it tightly and held it high. "Let me go or I'll stab you."

He just stared at her. Then one of his big gloved hands gave a quick twist and he snapped open a switchblade of his own. "You're getting it now."

With no choice left, Cassie charged him.

Linc pulled up in front of Cassie's house, switched off his ignition and hesitated. What if she simply told him to go home, that she was busy, that she didn't have time?

Then he would be a coward for refusing to face it, he decided. A damned coward. Besides, the niggling feeling that the outpouring of support might have infuriated the guy who was trying to frighten her wouldn't leave him alone, either. He'd seen bullies react that way, as if to justify their bad acts by making an even stronger statement.

A strange dynamic, but one with which he was all too familiar.

He climbed out of the truck. At once, though he couldn't say exactly what alerted him, he knew something wasn't right. He scanned the street but it looked normal except for an old pickup parked at the curb a few houses down.

But then he saw the shadows of two figures against the front kitchen curtains. She wasn't alone, and one shadow looked huge. Then he heard an unmistakable, muffled cry.

The clarity persisted. Get out or possibly die. Cassie, deprived of safe options, had no trouble taking action. She charged the man with her knife at the ready.

He reacted a little slowly, maybe because he misread her, and for one brilliant, hopeful moment, she thought she might make it. But just as she passed him, he grabbed her shoulder, shoved and threw her to the floor.

As she cried out, the knife slipped from her hand and she fell facedown, the wind knocked from her.

Oh, God, it was over now. Whatever he had intended, now he was probably mad. Panic filled her because she couldn't draw in air, and without air she couldn't move.

Still struggling to get her diaphragm to work, panic exploded even more as he grabbed her hair and yanked her head back so hard it hurt.

Death was coming. She knew it with absolute certainty.

At the same instant, she managed to drag in a breath, just as the world seemed to be darkening, and she heard a loud slam.

She opened her eyes to see Linc barreling through her front door, head and shoulders low like a football player ready to tackle. Her assailant let go of her hair.

Groaning, ignoring the pain in her neck and abdomen, she rolled over in time to see Linc on top of the man who had attacked her.

Then her entire focus of vision narrowed to the gleaming steel of the switchblade, still firmly gripped in the man's hand.

"Linc…" she barely croaked as she fought to get more air. She had to do something.

Struggling onto her hands and knees, she crabbed her way closer as Linc punched at the guy's head. The hand holding the knife came up, clearly aimed at Linc's side.

"No…" She launched herself with every ounce of strength she had, grabbing at the rising arm. The blade came perilously close to her face, but she didn't care. She had to save Linc.

Using her body's weight, she pressed the arm down. "He's got a knife."

Linc didn't answer, using his energy to punch the guy hard in the right shoulder. A hard punch, one that made the guy squeal. It also made him release the knife.

Quickly, Cassie shoved it away, and when it didn't go far enough, she shoved it again.

Linc let out an explosive puff of air as he took a punch himself from the other side, but he didn't let go of the man.

Cassie, finding energy again, clambered to her feet. She grabbed the switchblade, saw the chef's knife she had dropped and grabbed it, too. With a knife in each hand, she approached the struggling men.

Behind the ski mask, her assailant's eyes widened as he saw the knives in her hands.

"Can you hold him, Linc?" she asked in a voice threaded with ice. "Because I think I'd like to cut his throat."

Linc panted, "No. Call the cops. I've got him."

But all the fight seemed to have gone out of the guy at the sight of the two knives in Cassie's hands, or perhaps because of her icy tone of voice. Linc straddled his hips, legs tucked under the guy, and pressed both his shoulders to the floor.

"I take it you never wrestled," Linc said with something like satisfaction. "Don't twitch or I'll put you in a head-lock you'll never forget."

Later, the police and her assailant gone, Cassie felt near to collapse. Too much, she thought, and it was as if now the threat was past and safely removed, someone had pulled her plug. She was grateful, so grateful, when Linc wrapped her in his arms, held her almost painfully tight and mur-mured, "God, I was so scared for you."

She'd been scared for him, too, in those moments when he'd tackled the knife-wielding assailant. But as strength drained from her, she knew one thing for certain. There was no place she'd rather be than in Linc's arms. If only he felt the same way.

He offered her no options. He shepherded her back to her bedroom, helped her jam some clothing into a duffel, then urged her out to his truck. She didn't want to be alone, and apparently he didn't want to leave her alone.

Ever the white knight, she thought wistfully. If only he wanted her for more than that, but she had the heart-sickening feeling he did not. Struggling for some emotionally safe perch, she tried not to think about impending loss, tried to think about how she was going to manage to teach today, to help her students, without any sleep at all. Because she could tell there would be no sleep, not tonight.

That didn't distract her, so she tried to focus on her assailant. Anything to get rid of the lead in her heart and stomach. Even those moments of sheer terror.

"Do you think he would have killed me?" she asked finally.

"I don't know. He says not, and I think that's all we'll ever know."

"Yeah." She fell silent, trying to absorb the story that had excused all this insanity. "I have trouble believing his motivation." The man, Stan Bell, was a known alcoholic and ne'er-do-well who had a son on the basketball team. A team that looked like it had a good shot at the championship. Vic Bell, the son, had not been involved in the bullying, so it wasn't as if he might have lost his position on the team.

No, what had driven Stan Bell was that twenty years

ago he had been on a team headed for a championship, a team that had lost because the star player had gotten himself arrested just before the big game. Thus, Stan had been deprived of the win he had counted on, a win that probably would have been the high point of his entire life considering what had followed. All of this because he didn't want his own son to lose his chance at the trophy.

"It seems like an extreme reaction," Cassie remarked, forcing her focus away from the man beside her in the truck. Away from the need to fall into his arms and escape with him to a better place. "Really extreme."

"The man obviously has some serious mental-health issues."

And there it was going to have to stay, Cassie thought with a sigh. The guy was unbalanced. In his own mind he was probably being perfectly rational, but from the outside it looked insane.

"Just be prepared, Cassie," Linc said. "They're not going to be able to charge him with attempted murder. He didn't do enough."

"I know. Gage Dalton told me. He probably won't even go to jail for a whole year."

"Are you okay with that?"

"Do I have a choice? Maybe rehab will help him." She shook her head, wanting to put it all away, at least for now. She hurt, she was tired, and she wondered why she was going home with Linc when it was the stupidest thing in the world for her to do. If he'd wanted her the way she wanted him, he could have had her for the taking at her house. Except for that long, tight hug, there'd been no hint he wanted her.

He pulled up in front of his ranch. She knew he needed

to take care of his animals and she expected him to just usher her inside and leave her while he did that. It would fit.

But he astonished her. He wrapped her in a bone-crushing embrace the instant they stepped inside and whispered in her ear, "I was so afraid I'd lose you."

The sentiment touched her deeply, and she felt the crack in her heart, which had been aching steadily all day, grow wider.

But before she could respond to his embrace, he stepped back and held her by the shoulders, his electric blue eyes boring into hers.

"Tell me the truth, Cassie. Knowing that Bell might be on the streets again soon, are you going to stay or leave?"

There was no lying to that gaze, no evading the demand he was making. She knew exactly what he was asking and why. She also knew that he was making no promises.

But deep inside she knew something even more important: never in her life had it been this essential that she know exactly what she intended, and that she mean it with her whole being. She closed her eyes, to escape his stare, and searched her heart. The man who attacked her would walk these streets again. Maybe in a matter of weeks, maybe next year, but he was going to be back. He might even be crazier and madder then.

But a deep certainty filled her despite everything, and she'd never been more sure of herself in her life when she opened her eyes, met his intense gaze and said, "I'm staying. I'm here for good."

Something in his face softened. "For a while, anyway."

She shook her head. "No, I'm staying. This place has really grown on me. Today I found the kind of community I always wanted to be part of."

"In spite of Stan Bell?"

"Stan Bells exist everywhere. A community that will organize this fast to take care of the Carney family isn't easy to find."

A smile began to curve his mouth. "There's this other thing, too."

"What thing?"

"Me. I wear a few hats, which keeps me pretty busy, I admit. Coaching, teaching, this ranch. But I like my life. I'm not an ambitious sort of guy who wants to set the world on fire. I'm not going great places. I just want to be a good teacher, a good coach and a good steward to my land."

"What's wrong with that? Those are pretty important things. Look at me. I think teaching is a pretty high calling, myself. Now maybe I exaggerate my importance...."

Before she could finish, he hauled her close and silenced her with a deep, burning kiss. "You don't exaggerate your importance," he murmured huskily against her mouth when he let her catch her breath. "Six months."

"Six months?"

"Live with me until the end of the school year. Then if you can still stand it, I want to marry you. Because, damn it, I love you. I know it's fast. I'll give you time. But I've been falling in love with you since I first set eyes on you. I know I tried to stay away, but it was happening anyway. The way you move. The way you talk. You probably don't even realize how much attention I was paying to you. I thought I was being smart, but I was being stupid. I couldn't stop the inevitable. I love you, Cassie Greaves, and seeing you in danger tonight made it impossible for me to pretend any longer."

She felt her heart soar. Fast, maybe it was too fast, but

some part of her knew it with such certainty that denying it would be like cutting out her own heart. "I love you, too, Linc." She threw her arms around his neck, wanting him as close as she could get him, sure that she had at last found her place in life, in the world. With him. Happiness filled her, happiness beyond any she had ever known.

Later as they cuddled in bed together, he spoke. "I'm sorry I rushed in with all that. I suppose I could have chosen a better time, after all that happened to you tonight." He turned toward her, drawing her closer. "But I couldn't wait, Cassie. It already felt like I'd waited too long. When I was at the game, I was thinking I should have said something before I left. I had such a strong feeling we were getting our wires crossed."

"I guess we were," she sighed. "I really didn't think it was possible for anyone to love me. And then you thought I'd leave the way Martha did...."

"We need to learn to talk more. More clearly. Even about things we're afraid of."

She nodded against his shoulder, loving the feel of his skin against her cheek. "Kids?" she asked tentatively.

"Kids!"

For an instant she wondered if she'd asked the wrong question, but then his laugh rolled out, seeming to cover her like warm honey. "Definitely kids. I was going to wait before bombarding you on that. I definitely want at least two. Is that okay?"

"More than okay. I always wanted a large family."

"Well then. I've always wanted to hear kids running around and laughing in this house again."

He swooped in for a hard kiss, then lifted his head, gazing into her eyes. The bedside lamp was dim, but not too dim for her to see he'd grown very serious.

"I want this to be forever, Cassie. Forever."

So did she. Forever seemed like almost enough time.

\* \* \* \* \*

## COMING NEXT MONTH
### from Harlequin® Romantic Suspense
AVAILABLE NOVEMBER 13, 2012

### #1731 CHRISTMAS CONFIDENTIAL
*Holiday Protector* by Marilyn Pappano
*A Chance Reunion* by Linda Conrad
Two stories of private investigators hot on the trails of the women they love...just in time for Christmas!

### #1732 COLTON SHOWDOWN
*The Coltons of Eden Falls*
**Marie Ferrarella**
Tate Colton expected to take down the bad guys when he went undercover. But he never expected to fall for the woman he came to rescue.

### #1733 O'HALLORAN'S LADY
**Fiona Brand**
When evidence comes to light that Jenna's stalker is also linked with the death of ex-detective Marc's wife and child, he suddenly has a very personal reason to stay close.

### #1734 NO ESCAPE
**Meredith Fletcher**
To track down a serial killer, homicide detective Heath Boxer teams up with the latest victim's sister... and finds more than just a partner.

You can find more information on upcoming Harlequin® titles, free excerpts and more at www.Harlequin.com.

# REQUEST YOUR FREE BOOKS!
## 2 FREE NOVELS PLUS 2 FREE GIFTS!

 Harlequin®

## ROMANTIC
### SUSPENSE

**Sparked by Danger, Fueled by Passion.**

**YES!** Please send me 2 FREE Harlequin® Romantic Suspense novels and my 2 FREE gifts (gifts are worth about $10). After receiving them, if I don't wish to receive any more books, I can return the shipping statement marked "cancel." If I don't cancel, I will receive 4 brand-new novels every month and be billed just $4.49 per book in the U.S. or $5.24 per book in Canada. That's a saving of at least 14% off the cover price! It's quite a bargain! Shipping and handling is just 50¢ per book in the U.S. and 75¢ per book in Canada.* I understand that accepting the 2 free books and gifts places me under no obligation to buy anything. I can always return a shipment and cancel at any time. Even if I never buy another book, the two free books and gifts are mine to keep forever.

240/340 HDN FEFR

| | |
|---|---|
| Name | (PLEASE PRINT) |

| | |
|---|---|
| Address | Apt. # |

| | | |
|---|---|---|
| City | State/Prov. | Zip/Postal Code |

Signature (if under 18, a parent or guardian must sign)

### Mail to the **Reader Service:**
**IN U.S.A.:** P.O. Box 1867, Buffalo, NY 14240-1867
**IN CANADA:** P.O. Box 609, Fort Erie, Ontario L2A 5X3

Not valid for current subscribers to Harlequin Romantic Suspense books.

**Want to try two free books from another line?**
**Call 1-800-873-8635 or visit www.ReaderService.com.**

\* Terms and prices subject to change without notice. Prices do not include applicable taxes. Sales tax applicable in N.Y. Canadian residents will be charged applicable taxes. Offer not valid in Quebec. This offer is limited to one order per household. All orders subject to credit approval. Credit or debit balances in a customer's account(s) may be offset by any other outstanding balance owed by or to the customer. Please allow 4 to 6 weeks for delivery. Offer available while quantities last.

**Your Privacy**—The Reader Service is committed to protecting your privacy. Our Privacy Policy is available online at www.ReaderService.com or upon request from the Reader Service.

We make a portion of our mailing list available to reputable third parties that offer products we believe may interest you. If you prefer that we not exchange your name with third parties, or if you wish to clarify or modify your communication preferences, please visit us at www.ReaderService.com/consumerchoice or write to us at Reader Service Preference Service, P.O. Box 9062, Buffalo, NY 14269. Include your complete name and address.

HRS11B

## Special excerpt from Harlequin Nocturne

*In a time of war between humans and vampires,
the only hope of peace lies in the love between
mortal enemies Captain Fiona Donnelly
and the deadly vampire scout Kain....*

*Read on for a sneak peek at "Halfway to Dawn"
by* New York Times *bestselling author Susan Krinard.*

\* \* \*

Fiona opened her eyes.

The first thing she saw was the watery sunlight filtering through the waxy leaves of the live oak above her. The first thing she remembered was the bloodsuckers roaring and staggering about, drunk on her blood.

And then the sounds of violence, followed by quiet and the murmuring of voices. A strong but gentle touch. Faces…

Nightsiders.

No more than a few feet away, she saw two men huddled under the intertwined branches of a small thicket.

Vassals. That was what they had called themselves. But they were still Nightsiders. They wouldn't try to move until sunset. She could escape. All she had to do was find enough strength to get up.

"Fiona."

The voice. The calm baritone that had urged her to be still, to let him…

Her hand flew to her neck. It was tender, but she could feel nothing but a slight scar where the ugly wounds had been.

"Fiona," the voice said again. Firm but easy, like that of a man used to command and too certain of his own masculinity to fear compassion. The man emerged from the thicket.

He was unquestionably handsome, though there were deep shadows under his eyes and cheekbones. He wore only a shirt against the cold, a shirt that revealed the breadth of his shoulders and the fitness of his body. A soldier's body.

"It's all right," the man said, raising his hand. "The ones who attacked you are dead, but you shouldn't move yet. Your body needs more time."

"Kain," she said. "Your name is Kain."

He nodded. "How much do you remember?"

Too much, now that she was fully conscious. Pain, humiliation, growing weakness as the blood had been drained from her veins.

"Why did you save me? You said you were deserters."

"We want freedom," Kain said, his face hardening. "Just as you do."

Freedom from the Bloodlord or Bloodmaster who virtually owned them. But vassals still formed the majority of the troops who fought for these evil masters.

No matter what these men had done for her, they were still her enemies.

\* \* \*

*Discover the intense conclusion to*
*"Halfway to Dawn"*
*by Susan Krinard, featured in*
*HOLIDAY WITH A VAMPIRE 4,*
*available November 13, 2012,*
*from Harlequin® Nocturne™.*

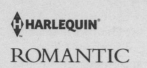

# HARLEQUIN®

## ROMANTIC
## SUSPENSE

**Get your heart racing this holiday season with double the
pulse-pounding action.**

# *Christmas Confidential*

## Featuring

### *Holiday Protector* by **Marilyn Pappano**

Miri Duncan doesn't care that it's almost Christmas. She's got bigger
worries on her mind. But surviving the trip to Georgia from Texas
is going to be her biggest challenge. Days in a car with the man
who broke her heart and helped send her to prison—private
investigator Dean Montgomery.

### *A Chance Reunion* by **Linda Conrad**

When the husband Elana Novak left behind five years ago shows up
in her new California home she knows danger is coming her way.
To protect the man she is quickly falling for Elana must convince
private investigator Gage Chance that she is a different person.
But Gage isn't about to let her walk away…even with the bad guys
right on their heels.

**Available December 2012 wherever books are sold!**

www.Harlequin.com

HRS27801